Oniaten Book I

The Shallows

by D.N. Wilkinson

The contents of this work, including, but not limited to, the accuracy of events, people, and places depicted; opinions expressed; permission to use previously published materials included; and any advice given or actions advocated are solely the responsibility of the author, who assumes all liability for said work and indemnifies the publisher against any claims stemming from publication of the work.

All Rights Reserved
Copyright © 2019 by D.N. Wilkinson

No part of this book may be reproduced or transmitted, downloaded, distributed, reverse engineered, or stored in or introduced into any information storage and retrieval system, in any form or by any means, including photocopying and recording, whether electronic or mechanical, now known or hereinafter invented without permission in writing from the publisher.

Dorrance Publishing Co
585 Alpha Drive
Suite 103
Pittsburgh, PA 15238
Visit our website at *www.dorrancebookstore.com*

ISBN: 978-1-4809-9128-6
eISBN: 978-1-4809-9104-0

Dedication

I dedicate this book to all my friends and family.

Too many to name, but there are two who deserve special recognition: my patient and wonderful wife, Melissa, and my dearest friend, Stephanie. Thank you both.

An additional thank you to the Native Americans who are continuing to preserve their identity. I hope this lets you know that you are not alone! If reality can't make things right then within this series, you will hopefully find at least some sense of what would have happened if the white man had been less of a monster.

A percentage of the proceeds from this and all future books I write will be donated to Native American charities. In the case of this book, they are split between NARF.org, the Native American relief fund, and also lakotanaap.org. I need to thank Evelyn Red Lodge and Marla Bull Bear for letting me know about them. Their mission is to keep foster parents of Native American children native. It is more important than anyone who isn't native can imagine.

While your purchase of this book aides them, they could use all the support you could provide. Think of these charities when you give. Thank you!

Preface

As the Native Americans came under increasing pressure from the European threat and the American Revolutionary War began to overrun their lands, Natives were forced to take sides, neither of which was beneficial to them as a society.

This book is meant to re-write history from 1779 to the present. If you will notice, however, there are two moons in this world, and per 'membrane' theory physicists, every version of reality exists somewhere in the Universe.

Until we can make it there, I present this book.

I choose to believe this universe exists.

A King Arthur for the people of the Americas!

I present the Oniaten!

Acknowledgements

The students and staff of the following school districts:
    Kennedy High School of Taylor (R.I.P ca. 2018)
    And a very special thanks to the students of Huron High School in New Boston who were so helpful in filling out characters and whose school grounds literally sit atop part of the scene that is portrayed in this series. We're still minus a moon, though…

Prologue

His first thought: 'Lie still, play dead. Hell, it's worked for me in the past.'

'Perhaps too well,' his inner voice reminded him.

Moving only his eyelids, as slowly as he could, he saw just enough to sense his surroundings.

Catching a glimpse of straw on the floor, red brick walls, and bars on the windows, he unwittingly whispered, "Well, shit!" —which he immediately regretted.

He lay still for a few more minutes. Not hearing or detecting any movement, he started to take stock of his physical condition.

Fingers and toes: check.

Feeling everywhere: check.

Cold, heavy iron on my wrists and ankles: check.

Lying on a slate of granite to which my shackles are bound…yep, that, too.

'So, look at it this way,' he said to himself, 'good news, bad news.'

I am awake, apparently have all my limbs, and can feel them. Score one for my side. 'Why am I shackled? Where in the hell am I, and how in the hell did I get here?' were his next thoughts. He wished these had not been such common questions throughout his life, but then, he mused, "Every day on this side of the sod, so they say!"

Fully alert and mobile now and sensing no guard presence, he found that there was enough slack for him to sit up on the slab of yellow granite. He could then make a better evaluation of his current abode.

He thought to himself, 'Really? A red brick with this yellow granite slab? The designer should be hanged!' A louder voice in his head said, 'He probably was.'

What he actually said aloud was a soft "hello." Not too loud; just loud enough for a nearby guard. Or much better yet, a nearby prisoner to hear.

"Hello," creaked a voice seemingly coming through an "air" grate close to the floor near the right wall.

"Hello," said Mitch again softly.

"Are you the one, the Ancient One?" creaked the voice in almost a death rattle. Not waiting for an answer, it continued louder and with more strength, "Native blood does not run through you, it runs to you, and you must continue to welcome it. To use it."

As if a whirlwind descended on Mitch's mind, every memory came back to him, of the sorrow and the joy, the triumph and the loss.

Remembering also the creaking voice, he replied aloud (too loud, in retrospect), "I am that, my friend, but believe me, it's not all it's cracked up to be!"

With a crash that would wake the dead, Mitch's cell door burst open.

Standing before Mitch in the doorway was what could only be described as a monolith, silhouetted against the first light he had seen since coming back to consciousness.

Pointing a bayonet at his throat, it asked, "Are you the one of the native blood?"

Mitch squeaked an answer as convincing as possible, "I have not a drop of native blood in me, not a single drop...upon my very life!"

The faceless monolithic inquisitor asked, "Are you not *the* Mitchell Garrett?"

In Mitch's mind, there was a little too much emphasis on 'the' in that sentence and, oh, yeah, 'What the hell has happened to me?' In his defense, and the only true answer he could give, he meekly said, "Well...I used to be."

The guard moved closer, his features becoming more clear in the fading light. A man Mitch thought could easily have been any of those he watched take up arms for their freedom, for a multitude of reasons, and die for those same reasons.

"What did you say?" the guard bellowed.

Mitch, unperturbed, patted the slab seat next to him and gently asked, "Do you have time for me to tell you a story?" Gazing around him and motioning toward the legion of bars, he said, "Because, apparently, I do."

The Darkening
Chapter One

One hundred and five years previously…

The earlier battle, the one at Niagara, had decimated the colonial defenses, and the cannon fire was just starting to quiet down as the day's battle came to a merciful end.

Captain Meltzer, who had been leading this small band of colonial soldiers, had unfortunately been one of the first causalities, which prompted Major Stewart to give Lieutenant Mitchell Garret a battle-field promotion to Captain and put him in charge of the regiment during battle.

Major Stewart was not really a leader, more of a political appointment, as Mitch reckoned. He looked quite dandy in his fresh officer's uniform, but for the life of him, Mitch couldn't remember seeing Stewart when Captain Meltzer was shot. Or anywhere else on the battlefield, for that matter.

Mitch, having been informed of his new position, tried to figure out where most of his troops had retreated. His immediate thoughts were to try to get them back to an organized, "get the hell out of here" kind of army.

The best part of this, he considered, was that he was ordered to lead his men off the field of battle and farther to the north and west under cover of darkness. Not into more bloodshed.

"Leave the tents, leave the fires burning, and let's get the blazes out of here before they know where we are going," Mitch said quietly to the smaller group of division leaders he had called to his side.

The plan seemed to work because the British retired for the night and were obviously planning the total domination of the field of battle the next day.

Mitch's plan was for there to be no army left to attack. "We move far enough west in the Pennsylvania territory, maybe even as far as the Ohio area at the Sandusky River. It will take them days to find us, and maybe General Washington's much promised reinforcements would arrive via ship at that well protected port." Mitch thought it unlikely to work, but it was as good a plan as he could come up with.

Right now, he needed to find Dieke.

Mitch continued to look for Dieke, only to be informed by a corporal that he had taken his surviving division to the west, just as the battle was ending for the day.

"Seems my old friend has some leadership ability about him, whether he wants to admit it or not. Of course, getting away from cannon fire is never a bad idea, no matter who you are," Mitch said aloud, but only to himself, by now no one was around to hear him, as they had already left to gather their men. The division leaders had their men prepared and were stoking the campfires to burn, if possible, perhaps, through the night.

Then the bugles signaled from both sides, announcing that all the wounded had been removed from the field, triggering the colonial army's action to start moving west along the path of the great lake. They moved quickly and as quietly as possible, and most importantly, away from those cannons.

'Perhaps we can get as far as Lake Erie's shore and the Port of Sandusky before they find us. Then hopefully a contingent of ships would be there to refresh their recently decimated force,' Mitch thought to himself.

He knew his luck was running low at this point, and the fact he was leading these men left him feeling more pity than confidence, considering this group. He knew who these men were. They were him a few years ago; tired of working Dad's farm, looking for something else to do with their lives, and all they had found was a cold and bloody battlefield for all their efforts.

While he considered himself a good engineer and very organized in his thoughts, he also thought his aggression level made him a better engineer than soldier. It was not the time now to debate that with himself; he had some asses to save. Chiefly his own.

Finishing fifteenth in a military school of thirty-five didn't give him a lot of confidence in his ability to keep anyone, including himself, alive.

Two years before this revolution had begun, Mitch had spurned his father's offer of running the farms in New York.

Truth be told, Mitch didn't particularly like farm life. The greater truth to be told here is that very few did. Especially those of his age. So, he was leading a group of, 'anything but working on the farm' men, which seemed oddly appropriate to him.

He thought himself more mechanically minded, and the British Miskatonic Pennsylvania Military Academy had engineering classes that interested him very much. He had excelled at the theory but had never taken the time to put any of it into practice when offered.

"Wish I had paid more attention before the war broke out," he said aloud again, to no one in particular.

When colonial officers took over the school after the war broke out, there was a sharp drop off in engineering teachers, and Mitch was disappointed that instead of building bridges and dams, he would be firing upon anyone wearing the red coat he once so desperately wished to wear.

They found a good campsite about five miles southeast of the major route along the lake. They built very small fires and kept their voices quiet. It was almost dawn and that would alert the redcoats to the fact that they no longer were facing an enemy, but a bunch of empty tents and ashy, glowing embers.

Morning At Niagra

"Goddamn it!" Colonel Arrington said.

As they worked their way across the former colonial camp, his guard always careful of an ambush out from the encroaching wild fauna that surrounded them.

"Where in the hell are they?"

His assistant, Major Timmons, merely shrugged and said, "It appears they were not ready to fully engage us yet, sir."

"To hell with them," Arrington said. "Bring out the locals, the natives, and find them! They can't be many hours ahead of us! The less ready they are, the better for us."

The redcoats formed marching lines, and as soon as it was daylight, they began heading west along the lake shore of what was called by the locals Erie.

Arrington looked across the misty waters and thought, '*Eerie* would be a better name.'

The mist on the water seemed to have a mind of its own, and it also seemed to be following them, Arrington noticed this, but refused to mention, as it must be an illusion, he shakily convinced himself.

THE BATTLE OF SANDUSKY

The colonials had moved quickly, being smaller in number and scared out of their wits, arriving at a place north of the Pennsylvania Colony. Mitch noticed some of his men called it the Dutch Colony and yet others had begun to call it the Ohio Territory.

They had found the highest ground they could. They travelled some ways north onto unnamed ground, until they reached a large breach in a strong river that fed Lake Erie.

Then they waited, hoping against hope that the redcoats would continue west and give them a chance to regroup.

The 'high ground,' if you could call it such, being a rise above a ditch and some thorny, bushy patches that were unfortunately all the colonial soldiers had to hide behind.

The drizzly weather didn't help with comfort much, but it did help with what they called 'cover,' adding a degree of haze to the potential battlefield.

The spotty fog served as better guise than anything the land had to provide in this area, even as far as the coast.

Mitch knew he should move farther inland for safety but still was holding out hope for replacements off a ship, perhaps two, from the great lake. Though, he admitted to himself, the time between a battle and replacements seemed to be getting longer by the battle.

As night of the next day began to fall, the colonials could hear the marching, could hear the commands, and knew that the stalling plan had reached its unfortunate conclusion.

The Brits, it appeared, had camped just on the eastern side of the river. They were stopping for the day, it seemed, and had not yet noticed them.

As daylight formed, this illusion deteriorated rapidly. Lines of men in red stood on the eastern banks of the Sandusky, though many fewer than Mitch had anticipated.

Mitch viewed his own forces and those of the redcoats and thought, 'We might just be able to win this skirmish, or at least give us time to retreat to better ground again.' Then the lead started to fly. Cannon fire and its ever-present shrapnel from both sides laid waste to the mass of humanity that had rushed forward to meet each other in battle.

Mitch, at better than six feet tall and carrying what he told himself was just a few extra pounds, was in no position to hide.

Still he rose to look over the battlefield. 'Much too much red down there,' he thought. With all the casualties, he had figured that the British line would weaken, but natives seemed to fill in any gaps the colonials had created in the Brit lines. There was seemingly no end of natives, he reflected.

Uniforms of the Brits and the blood of men from both sides were coloring the resulting field of battle a disturbing shade of crimson.

He looked around and finally saw the unwieldy mess of blond hair belonging to Lieutenant Dieke Carson, his second in command and best friend.

The best trapper, fighter, and…well…person to have around when rations ran short, or sadly, did not show up at all.

Mitch grabbed Dieke by the shoulder and pulled him away from the rise. "Well, Dieke," Mitch said, "I thought we had this battle won until the natives joined the fray." Pointing in the direction of the redcoats' line, he continued, "They must have been waiting across the river until we could adequately engage our men. More to shoot at, I suppose," Mitch said absentmindedly.

Dieke was a little taller, maybe stronger than Mitch would like to admit. While not a genius, he was the best man Mitch had ever fought beside and a friend since the Academy, to boot. Most importantly, someone he would die to protect and knew would do the same for him.

The boys had grown up mere miles from each other, but had never interacted because Mitch was, after all, just a farmer's son, and Dieke was the first son of a wealthy, by colonial terms, business owner.

They had kind of known of each other, but more through reputation and glances across the gathering of businesses that could almost be described as a city.

There had been no introductions until Miskatonic and the military school, where they shared stories of having seen each other but never bothered to go across the way to say hello.

Dieke's father, as Mitch remembered him, was a very respectable man, but a bit of a bore as Dieke had described him.

As far as he knew, they hadn't spoken in years, perhaps decades.

Mitch recalled that Dieke's "formal education" involved paying brothel bills and signing land agreements that he never fully understood, but he made wiser decisions now based upon that past experience. Mitch was most confident in Dieke's ability to not make the same mistake twice, although Dieke did truly believe that it was never a mistake to visit a brothel. 'No one is perfect,' Mitch reminded himself. Smiling as he remembered the stories Dieke had told; half of which he figured might be the truth.

Mitch's own parents had passed while he was away at school. They had told him that it was an unavoidable tragedy as the war front moved to and fro. Little consolation. A lingering need, perhaps even a demand for revenge, remained in his mind, but where best to direct that?

The British?

The natives who sided with them?

The loyalists who hid amongst them?

He could not quite nail that down.

The stories always seemed sketchy and the methods of their deaths varied; worst of all, they were always told from less-than-reliable sources.

Dieke, who would be a reliable source, did not seem up to talking about it and would shy away from having the conversation, occasionally becoming angry at the very mention of it.

That had, if anyone had asked, weakened Mitch deep down somehow. When he allowed himself the luxury of thoughts of justice, and yes, perhaps vengeance, knowing whom to blame was most important. At this point, he was willing to blame everyone.

He was slammed back to reality as the sound of a gunshot, much too close, made him view the battlefield anew.

He turned to Dieke and said, just loud enough for Dieke to hear. "I hate to question our soldiers' abilities, but the odds here aren't lookin' great."

Dieke looked over the shrub that was separating them, protection as it were, and softly said, "Mitch, do you think you can outrun an arrow?"

Mitch looked at Dieke, looked again at the field of battle, looked at the colonial "line of defense," and said, not in a whisper, but more in a soft statement, "I'd rather not have to find out Dieke. Honestly, I'd rather not!"

Dieke looked at his, now, captain. A friend for almost four years and an acquaintance, you might say, since birth. They really connected a couple of years before the war started when Dieke, rather than face a mountain of debt and his father's unwillingness to pay that debt, acquiesced to his dad's insistence he make something of himself and had thus enrolled in the Miskatonic Pennsylvania Military Academy as a peace offering that would cover his debts.

When he first arrived, Mitch had been there a month or so and had just turned seventeen years old. Dieke remembered this clearly because he himself was sixteen years, eleven months, and seven days old; a fact Mitch would never let him forget. The good-natured jesting displayed only helped to bond them, as they were both new to this. 'Mitch ready to learn everything he could, especially the difficult stuff,' Dieke thought. 'Why would anyone want to learn engineering and the numbers and the building of stuff and things?'

Dieke had joined as much to get away from his father's business as to learn anything really new. He could shoot a gun with the best of them and had killed more than his share of game. Each time he returned home with a deer he would later butcher, his father would say, "If you had been at my shop today, you could have made enough money to buy two of those!" Dieke felt that this, more than anything, was the difference between him and his father.

Mitch, on the other hand, was far more fascinated by new technology, by new ways of not just waging war, but of running a city, a country even. Dieke had sat for many a night and listened to Mitch's plans for grist and lumber mills, for repeating firearms, and another dozen or so things Dieke couldn't remember right now, nor was likely to anytime soon.

Dieke also remembered when the war broke out. When their British military instructors, especially in engineering, were quickly removed to the front, and colonial soldiers, ready to wage a revolution, had taken control of the school. That's when Mitch and everything else, had changed.

Chapter Two

The view from the other side of the battlefield looked much the same to British Colonel Rupert Arrington. The odds, however, looked considerably better.

He looked up from his spyglass and turned to the Native on his immediate left.

'Gert' was the common name around camp for him; they also called him 'medicine man,' though Rupert still didn't think him any more than a savage; just another one who had sided with the British in a much-needed show of strength in the West, holding out for any chance at retaining their land…or so they had been led to believe. Arrington had no idea of the reasoning and didn't really care.

"I say," the Brit spoke, "medicine man, I cannot believe that your chief is right there in the midst of the fighting. I mean look at me up here, safe but overlooking the action and directing my men by messenger. The way a civilized soldier, an officer even, conducts battle."

Amazed at first at the fact the Brit had called him 'medicine man,' Gert came to himself and replied, "That is why he is our chief," looking at the field of battle himself.

Colonel Arrington looked through his spyglass yet again. "This bloody mess will be over soon enough, medicine man, soon enough," he said, spurring his horse away from the view, toward refreshments and his tent.

Left alone Gert looked out over the field below him. He could not comprehend how this slaughter could ever be over until everyone was gone. What he said aloud after the retreating officer was, "If you say so, Colonel."

As quietly as possible, and with all the stealth he had learned from his childhood, Gert snuck down, away from the retreating officer and closer to the fighting.

The cover here consisted of some weeds and what could generously be called a ditch.

He prepared his bow, taking as much care as he had with any shot that he had ever taken in his life. He loaded the arrow, knew it to be the correct one by the arrow's tip glowing faintly green in the dreary light.

Meanwhile, back across the field of the battle, the colonial line was being violently pushed back.

Mitch was more offended than afraid; hand-to-hand fighting and heartbeat to literally last heartbeat…such a waste of good men.

He glanced past the dead that lay all around and saw Dieke and that volunteer French corporal from Monroe (he thought his name was Masarant or something like that). Between them the captive chief of the native force struggled in their grasp; they had taken him alive!

'Finally, some good luck for us,' Mitch thought. 'A high-ranking prisoner might keep us alive a little longer.' Dieke's eyes widened as he looked on, and he seemed to jump as he was hit by a shot to the upper leg; well, frankly, his ass, Mitch had to admit. The chief took that moment to try to gain control from his captors. Mitch rushed over in an attempt to keep the chief from fleeing back to the redcoats' line.

As he ran to the scene, he felt a stabbing pain in his shoulder and back, then his chest, then…well, then, he didn't feel anything anymore.

Unintended Consequences

Gert looked on from his location; first with satisfaction, then with horror. His arrow flew true and would have struck Chief Quay Quay right in the heart before he could be taken away by the colonials or the redcoats. Instead, some blue-coated idiot stepped in front of the chief and took the most sacred arrow of the tribe in what appeared to be near his right shoulder blade.

The chief, breaking free of his now-single captor, stared at the arrow lodged in Mitch's back and looked up across the field (a knoll, really) from its obvious direction of release.

His eyes and Gert's met for just a moment before Gert ducked down and out of sight…too late, he feared.

While all this was bad enough and something to be dealt with, Gert's even greater fear was his sister. "KT is never going to forgive me for this!"

From Gert's perspective, it had hit the man to the right side of his spine, the man in a blue uniform, not that colors meant much, but being ostensibly on the redcoat's side now caused Gert renewed pause. Gert chanced another look at the scene.

The stricken man turned and looked at Gert as he rose across a field of the dead, the dying, and the screaming. Dead to this world, he locked eyes with the medicine man.

Eyes burning through Gert's soul….and a lot of his last and his next ones, too, he felt. Then collapsed to the ground. "Oops" was all Gert could mutter!

As the British and native forces took the field and the battle, Colonel Arrington rode up to Chief Quay Quay. The chief was still staring at the body of Mitch, arrow tip visible and ever so faintly glowing.

Arrington said, "Come along, Chief, let's leave the dead in peace."

The field lay quiet.

A few colonials were identifying and cataloging their dead while the British watched. This was, after all, to be a civilized war, was it not?

When they had completed this task, they would join the retreating force. Night would soon fall, the wounded tended or evacuated, and in the morning, their army would again be on the move, Arrington surmised.

As Colonel Arrington looked on, he turned to his aide de' camp and declared, "All noncombat natives are to return to their grounds to the west. They may come before morning and retrieve their dead, as is their custom. Make sure the chief knows this and that he will remain with us and under our protection."

The aide obediently turned and rode toward the Indian encampment to relay the orders.

Night had fully fallen as Jethro, who was always near the medicine man when he was in battle by orders of the great chief, looked about him in the darkness.

From those left behind in the battle, the British and natives, Jethro had to admit, had proven victorious. However, looking at the scene of the carnage of every color, stripe, and creed, his slow but steady mind thought, "Did anyone really win here? Is there any honor to be found?"

They were out here looking for the man Gert had shot, and that was all he was told. Really all he needed to know, he admitted.

His malaise was interrupted by a shrill whisper. If such a thing could be done, KT could do it…to perfection, in fact.

KT, which was short for something she did not wish spread far and wide, was daughter of the chief; and every bit as important, sister of the medicine man Gert, to whom she was shrilly whispering, "What did he look like again, there sure shot? Where did you see him? What rank did he appear to be?" KT implored Gert for more information.

Gert said with as much irony as he could muster, "Like a white man in a blue uniform, sister! He should have dropped right where the high ground begins to recede to the east." He pointed in the general area they were looking.

KT looked at him in the darkness, with more than derision. Perhaps an ancient curse or a younger sister's remembrances of pulled hair, she simply said, "Did you happen to notice his hair color, by chance?"

Gert, without emotion, replied, "Dark, but not as dark as ours."

"Well, that narrows it down a little." 'A very little,' KT had to concede to herself.

As the three wandered among the fallen, it was very difficult not to trip and slip, either over bodies or through mud holes, made red with blood and gore.

Jethro spoke next. "Look over there. See the glow? It must be your arrow, medicine man!"

As the three looked in the direction Jethro had indicated, a faint, almost too faint to see, greenish glow was emanating from the back of the body of a soldier in blue.

They approached slowly and looked down upon the body.

Jethro turned to KT and said, as much as asked, "Well, we found him, now what?"

'Now what, indeed,' thought KT.

"Sure can't leave him here to be buried in a mass grave with the others; or worse yet, sent home to the family plot. Hope no one ever has to see that," KT intoned, shuttering from more than the cold and dampness.

"Let's get him out of here as a native victim and back to our encampment! We will discuss it further then, but right now, let's just get all four of us out of here before a whole lot of very difficult questions are asked."

Chapter Three

The exercise of moving the limp body in blue was made no easier by the sudden downpour of rain nor by the uphill climb to their little piece opposite the battlefield.

At least the body wouldn't float away if they dropped him, physics suggested.

Jethro said, looking up into the torrent, just loud enough for KT to hear him, but not Gert, "I don't think the old ones are very happy with us right now."

KT pretended not to hear, but had to admit the thought had crossed her mind as well.

Having arrived at the temporary roundhouse, they brought the body inside. The rest of the native dead were left neatly assembled in rows near the edge of the native compound for movement west come morning.

The soldier's body was now wrapped in the native cloth of those braves killed in the battle. The three sat in front of his prone form, first looking at the wrapped body, then at each other and then back again.

Finally, KT broke the silence and said, "Well, I suppose Gertrude here," gesturing toward Gert, the medicine man, "should be the one to tell him."

Gert, mildly infuriated at the use of his full first name, stared at his sister and said, through gritted teeth and more as a curse than a statement, "I merely let the arrow fly; it is you, dear sister Karvenia Tallywag, who should tell him since you made us bring him here."

Despite a level of tension an outsider would have been knocked unconscious by, both knew this quite well.

'Grandfather is going to be none too happy, and there was plenty of the blame to go around,' KT thought. The British, the colonists, the loyalists, the tribes, as their alliances found a home among one of the factions; their father for choosing a side, her brother, for firing the arrow, and finally her. Who, in desperation, knew nothing else to do nor anyone else left to blame.

Looking upon it, she decided she had made the easiest decision but also the bravest and would ultimately, unless something even more bizarre occurred, be bound to it/him forever. "And a day," she said aloud.

Jethro and Gert both heard the utterance, the silence had been so eternal it seemed, and almost in a single voice they said, "What?"

"Just doing some figuring in my head. We have two weeks and a day to get him back. We must put his body under the others when we load the carts; can't let his uniform be spotted."

She considered their faces and hoped their belief in her superior "education" would convince them of the timing and that they did not see the fear behind her eyes; both on him remaining inanimate long enough to get home and not noticed by any nosy redcoats.

In honesty she knew it was less than a two-week movement of the two moon cycles; about thirteen sunrises, best she could remember.

"Going to be close; let's hope for good, cool weather."

Their conversation was halted as a very elderly man was greeted and led into the roundhouse, the name the white men gave the curved, elongated structures. More permanent settlements in the West had used bigger ones that were known as longhouses, mostly due to the supply of white shag birch bark available and a plentiful supply of hides making these the strongest and most simple to put up in a hurry and reinforce as needed through the seasons.

The ones here were much smaller and much less "birchy" is how Jethro would describe it. They served the purpose but would not last for long and weren't meant to.

The battle lines would probably be moving east. The medicine man and his sister would return with their grandfather and the native dead to their lands in the Northwest, which was along a different river, a long way from anything resembling a "white man's" civilization.

Their father, the true chief, would stay with the remaining force of native braves as long as they could be of service, the Brits had apparently decided. The British were very business-like in this matter, as well.

As a bonus, a contingent of wounded or cowardly British soldiers and colonial prisoners, as well as allied natives, would accompany them along the trail, to be placed too far away from the action to be a problem, even if they did escape.

To KT the irony that where she called home was where they were sending prisoners as banishment was not lost. She was both amused and angered by it. 'Perhaps it was both things to both,' she waxed philosophically.

To the British soldiers, it was flat out punishment, and that made her smile, despite the commotion of Grandfather coming in. The three stood.

"Great Chief Chewachta, we are honored by your presence!" Gert bowed in a grand gesture.

"For the love of the elders, Gertrude, get out of my way and sit down!" the great chief said. 'Gertrude, twice in one day, was more than two too many times!' he thought. Nonetheless, he smiled, bowed again, and sat down.

Great Chief Chewachta looked down at the blue uniformed officer that Jethro was unwrapping at KT's urging motions.

"You know who I blame for all of this?" He paced unevenly and looked around the room at the three guilty faces, each hoping it wasn't them. "I blame myself and your grandmother for coddling your father!"

'The look of astonishment on the faces of those three cannot be adequately put into words," Chewachta thought to himself, hiding a smile he had hidden for ages.

"Let us prepare for our trip back, Karvenia. Keep track of the days, and I will do what I can to keep us moving quickly. If it happens along the way, we will think these current problems but trifles."

Chapter Four

The trip home, thank the elders, went well, and took just about exactly as long as KT had predicted. Owing it more to luck and her Grandfather than her education. She would of course take the credit anyway.

They gently placed the dead braves in their ceremonial areas and with the families. The dead colonial at this point was considered part of the chief's family and was carried into KT's quarters, the largest longhouse on the reservation, as it also served the great elder chief and the medicine man Gert.

Jethro stood tall and imposing—statuesque, perhaps—at the opening of the doorway, maintaining the flow of people in and out of the great chief's longhouse. 'This evening we will figure out what to do,' KT hoped.

Chewachta had remained close to the British guards during the trip back, trying to keep them as far away from the dead colonial as possible. He still had a few questions. After a lively discussion of the facts that could only be described as brutal in an overall sense, this is what Great Chief Chewachta knew: Gert, the medicine man and, incidentally, his grandson, had accidently shot a colonial fighter instead of the real target, which was to be his son, the true Chief Quay Quay, Gert and KT's dad.

The chief was being held with the British contingent to maintain order among the natives, whom the British had been utilizing as basically a tactical team and, when necessary, as "cannon fodder."

Chewachta knew the situation he was in…they were in.

It was best that they had taken the body with them and quite clever of KT to go about it the way she did.

The Brits were a little squeamish when it came to blood and assorted other events that happen upon death and had avoided the "death cart," as they termed it.

Chewachta looked KT in the eyes and said, "You made the only decision that could have been made; smart to bring him back here and to keep him with our fallen warriors."

In his mind ran the thoughts: 'This poor white man is going to have a hell of a time first believing, then coming to terms, with this. Then, and only then, he will learn how to use it." No small task for any human—native or otherwise.

Then, on a brighter note, he knew that eventually the power within him, the Oniaten, would be very instrumental in instructing and motivating this man.

"KT, how many days have passed since the shot killed the soldier?" Chewachta asked.

"Fifteen days," KT replied. "Give or take a few hours."

Grand Chief Chewachta had a look of horror on his face at the timing he had just received. Turned sharply toward KT, he said, "Well, that was certainly cutting it close; great decision with so little room for error, KT. The elders have indeed blessed us, assuming this man comes back as we believe he will."

Chewachta finished, "KT, you and Gert will be at his side now; most importantly when he rises. That is when the real training starts!" This time he stared at Gert, who did not raise his eyes to meet his grandfather's.

"I guess we are about to find out what your soldier and you can handle."

The look on Chewachta's face showed more amusement than concern; not a laughing matter by any stretch, but the first time a white man must learn everything from the beginning, from a stranger who is a native, no less.

That may take a while, perhaps more than one lifetime.

That was KT and Gert's job at the moment…

However, it was still Gert's missed arrow that caused all of this.

He turned to Gert and said briskly but not loudly, "You know, Gert, you were not to let that arrow fly at anyone but a native."

Without waiting for reply, he continued, "You will provide protection, food, and anything else KT asks for while we awaken our white man!"

"Let's hope he can be convinced," he said, looking KT in the eyes again, "to be the warrior to save us, considering we were the ones to 'kill' him."

He gave another sharp look at Gert, who met his eyes this time and could not help but think to himself, 'Why does every good deed I try to do become a mess? I swear I can get everything right and still make things worse.' He looked at the body in front of him and shook his head slowly and looked down, finally saying, "As you wish, Great Chief!"

Chewachta again looked around at all of them. "No one will be allowed to enter this roundhouse but you three. Well, including the guard Jethro and our soldier, five, I suppose." He pointed at the prone form on the bench, "I will make that clear!"

KT and Gert watched as the great chief left the roundhouse, looked at each other, and had they had the fluency of the common British turn of phrase, would have said, 'Oh, shit, what now?' or something to that general effect.

Jethro, who had been in the roundhouse room during the entire conversation, said, "Well, he is probably gonna be hungry and thirsty after being dead and all, do you not think?"

"Well, we'll see how he's feeling when he re-awakens. I have heard sometimes the undead never eat again," KT responded, more with hope than conviction.

The Awakening
Chapter Five

Despite the description the spell had predicted, the spirit within Mitch began to awaken in exactly fifteen days. He awoke quite slowly and could not use his current host to look around him yet. "Best to take stock of myself before insisting this human—I guess it's a human—wakes up."

The spirit's memory had started to return to him, and he remembered his name.

'Oniaten is what I was called,' he clearly remembered now. I was undead, but it appears I have been just dead for a long time. How long he would have to figure out when he woke up this soldier. 'Ah, a soldier, he is a warrior,' the Oniaten said to himself as he realized he could consider the host's mind and see his memories. 'Funny thing is he seems to have few images of himself in his memory. Without a mirror, I am unable to envision this warrior's features.' But from the memories he was conjuring up, he knew this man to be non-native.

'Perfect,' he thought. 'The new champion of the dead, the new Native messiah, appears to be European with self-esteem issues. This could potentially be a problem, but only if he fights me on it. From what I can see from his memories, he will offer little resistance once he understands his options. I will be sure to explain that to him as soon as he is awake and alert.'

The Oniaten then began to more closely examine his own memories, trying to figure out exactly how he was killed, when that should not have been possible. His strongest memory was him being very sick with one of the diseases of the swamp area his tribe had been forced to hide in. The face of a warrior looking down on him. He remembered clearly the warrior in full paint and full battle gear, but he also remembered she was clearly a woman; a woman with bluish-gray eyes, which he recollected finding odd in a native. Still he remembered her reaching down and placing her hands on his face. He then remembered his disease, infirmity…even his pain going away. He also remembered his heart had quit beating just before that had occurred.

He continued to re-evaluate his host's history, mining the memories of this man who seemed to call himself Mitch, though others in his memories called him captain or sir; recent memories, the Oniaten was sure.

One case in particular stood out: his recent promotion where he was first referred to as Captain Mitchell Garrett.

'This just keeps getting better,' the Oniaten said, but without sarcasm, merely with the knowledge that this was probably not going to be the smoothest transition for Captain Mitch.

'It's been two moon cycles; I think I can handle him awake now. Let me see if I can rouse him,' the elder spirit reasoned.

Quietly, as if gently waking a sleeping child, the Oniaten said to Mitch in his brain: 'Time to wake up, sleepy head.' This had no effect, so he yelled into his brain, 'Soldier, wake up now!' Even this didn't have any effect, so he tried one more thing. 'Captain Mitchell Garrett, you are to come to attention at this moment!'

On the outside of Mitch's mind, his handlers looked worried and confused.

"I do not understand this; the two moons have cycled, so he should have awoken two days ago!" KT said almost in a panic.

A panic not shared by Gert, who still hoped something had gone wrong with the magic, or the arrow didn't go deep enough; anything that would allow him to just bury this white man, forget it all, return to the fight and get his father back!

As if magic itself had heard his thoughts, the coverings on the 'revolutionary' soldier as the captured colonials seemed to call themselves, slowly began to twitch where his hands had been placed across his chest.

Gert went outside quickly, opening the flap that served as a door, briefly illuminating the dimly lit space, to have Jethro inform the great chief.

KT slowly rose from her stool and approached the prone "body."

The movements were more active now but still nothing to be afraid of... she hoped. "Just relax now," she spoke out loud to the restive corpse.

At her words Gert and Jethro charged back into the longhouse, a knife in Gert's hand and a drawn bow in Jethro's.

KT looked at them sternly and motioned them to put their weapons down. "What good do you think those would do? Seriously?"

Gert and Jethro appeared to consider this and relax a little.

Moving closer Gert asked, "Has he had made any noise yet?"

KT, running out of patience with her brother after this weeks-long vigil, said, "Why, yes, he was just singing one of the latest arias from Europe before you came back in."

Gert gave her an evil look. "I may not know what an aria is, but I do know what a bitc…"

He was cut off by a loud moan from under the shroud. It wasn't like any moan the three had ever heard.

"It was almost so loud you couldn't hear it," KT would later recall.

Jethro took a quick look outside. Reservation life continued as normal. No one else appeared to have noticed anything, and then he saw Great Chief Chewachta staring at him from the smooth, rocky banks of the river. The chief nodded slowly to Jethro as he approached and spoke briefly, waved him away, and went back to talking to the "braves-in-training," as the Brits had called the younger of the tribe.

Jethro came back into the doorway after this brief interaction with Chewachta. Resuming his duties of blocking it from any intruders, he leaned his head into the longhouse and said, "No one else seems to have heard it but the great chief."

"Is he coming soon? What did he say?" KT asked frantically.

"He looked at me and nodded and continued his talks," Jethro replied, knowing she would not take that bit of news well.

"That's it?"

"Remember, dear sister, he told you the colonial was ours. Ours to raise and to teach, like a child, really. Congratulations, Karvenia Tallywag, it appears it's a boy! Quite a large one at that!"

Gert couldn't resist a smile and a jab back at her for the Aria nonsense. 'I really should ask what that means one day,' he thought to himself.

Then the covering began to move actively. Jethro moved away from the entrance but kept his eyes on it. He and Gert stood close enough to be of help restraining him, if that were possible, or necessary, but out of his sight. KT should to be the first one he saw.

KT let out an audible sigh and began to slowly unwrap the body. 'Is it a body anymore?' thought KT. 'Is it a human? Is it dead or undead?'

"Well we know from those who identified him, according to father's dispatches," she said to the men, "that he is a Captain Mitchell Garrett of the Miskatonic Pennsylvania Mountain Military Academy."

"I suppose for now we should call him captain and not think about the rest," she said, allowing for Gert and Jethro's edification, her inner voice reasoned.

As she continued to unwrap the "captain," she noticed he seemed to be trying to help, but feebly at best.

Apparently it would take a while for the joints to start to work again after being "dead still" for the dual moon cycle, plus a few too many days.

KT couldn't resist the mental pun; couldn't quite shake the literalness of it either. Things are about to get incredibly difficult and, even worse, chaotic if anything goes wrong.

The words of the Great Chief echoed in her head: 'He's yours now!' It was all up to her and Gert now.

Let's hope he is a reasonable and open-minded white man.

Though, she had to admit, those men seemed to be as mythical as the Mukwa, the SpiritBear the Elders spoke of.

Chapter Six

Mitch's eyes remained closed, and the only things he was actually moving were his arms and legs, in a deliberate attempt to help 'them' uncover him.

He remained in his colonial officer's uniform, although for some reason, his boots were apparently missing.

KT had noticed that when they un-loaded him off of the cart after the trip here from Sandusky. She figured they were stolen during the trip, but it shouldn't be hard to find the culprit; he'll be the native wearing colonial officer's boots.

Plus, she was awfully sure this captain, when awakened fully, would be in no mood for theft or forgiveness.

Jethro said, "Look, KT, he is trying to talk; his eyes are opening. Get over him!"

KT leaned over the man and helped to wipe away some of the crust from his eyes.

He seemed to open them fully and focus for the first time. He looked up and could make out a face; no features, really, but it was a person, for sure. He croaked out a "What…"

KT leaned closer and said, "Good morning, Captain, did you enjoy your rest? Are you hungry or thirsty?"

Mitch stared at the figure trying to concentrate and get his voice working.

When his voice did finally work, it bellowed, "Where in the hell am I, and who in the devil are you?"

He tried to get up but had almost no success. Drained, he lay back down, still trying to focus.

As the face came closer again, his vision had cleared, and he considered the face of a most beautiful Native Indian woman. A light appeared to surround her head.

'Surely a goddess,' he thought, but that perhaps would not do her justice in this moment.

She was saying something, but he wasn't listening. He could not look away from the form in front of him. At that moment, he felt that he had known her forever.

She shook him and asked again, "Are you hungry? Thirsty? Is there anything I can get you?"

The trance broken enough to allow him to think. He said, "Not really; we just had mess before the fighting began. Still full from that slop, I guess."

"About that…" KT said. "That slop you had for mess was almost a month ago. You have had neither food nor water in almost eighteen days. I'm gonna get you some broth just to moisten your

insides a little."

Mitch found the strength to sit up, but finding the mental capacity to comprehend the fact, or rather purported fact, that he had slept and not eaten for eighteen days was sinking in very slowly.

Mitch, in a more civilized tone, asked again, "Where am I, and who are you?"

"Excellent questions. I'll answer the second one first," the goddess answered. "You will call me KT. I am the daughter of the warrior chief of our tribal confederacy."

"This," pointing to Gert, "is my brother and the tribe's medicine man. You may refer to him as Gert or medicine man.

"And this," motioning toward Jethro, "is our own personal army when necessary and our great friend always," smiling a sisterly smile toward him, "Jethro.

"Now as to where you are. You are currently in my longhouse on our reservation; far to the northwest and a fortnight's travel from any fighting. A prisoner of war camp for some; for me it is home. For you it will be more a training ground."

'Perhaps someday he will think of it as his home, as well,' KT thought.

Mitch started to interrupt, but KT held up her hand and continued. "We know you are Captain Mitchell Garrett of the Miskatonic Pennsylvania Mountain Military Academy Militia." She paused, looked at him, and shook her head a little. "I really would have shortened that name myself, but I was told to be respectful.

"Anyway," she continued, "I know this information from your fellow officers who positively identified your body. I am afraid, Captain Garett, you are dead…for the most part."

Mitch smiled very nicely at KT and said, "Fair maiden," he reached for her hand, squeezed it tightly, then very tightly, and screamed, "What in the bloody hell happened to me, and what in the hell are you talking about?"

He released her hand just before he broke her bones, feeling a strength he knew his hand had not previously possessed. He rubbed his hands together and looked to KT.

Gert and Jethro both came to her defense just as he released her hand.

KT, too, was rubbing her hand, and Gert was beside her. "No bones broken thankfully," she said to Gert.

"This time," Gert said, glaring at the white man, or thing, or whatever it had become.

Even by his own hand, his own magic, he had no clear definition of what he had accidentally created.

"I could never hurt you badly, KT," Mitch said out of nowhere as he stared at her.

In his head, for some reason, he knew deep inside, to kill her would kill a part of him. "But I am already dead, is that right?" he asked after what he felt too long a silence. "Am I right?" he screamed into what seemed to him an abyss.

His whole body seemed to suddenly lose strength, and he went limp, though his eyes still probed for more information.

"Let's get some soup in you and see if something familiar will help. When you are fully awake, we will tell you the whole story, and the destiny you have fallen, or rather been pushed, into." KT glared at Gert as she spat out the words.

"You are the first white man to be given this (though the word 'given' seemed out of joint as she said it, even the 'first' part was a little iffy to Mitch), and it will not be easy, but you must trust us." She motioned to herself, then to Gert, and she lifted his head till he met her eyes. "If you don't trust us, you will just be a dead man walking."

Chapter Seven

Mitch took the carved wooden knurled (he believed it was called), cup of broth he was handed, and tried a spoonful. It had very little taste, and the taste it had was bitter.

KT noticed his facial expression and said, "Well, at least you have some taste apparently. I was afraid you would have none at all." She added hopefully, "Perhaps it will even improve over time?"

The way Mitch saw it, it had plenty of room for improvement. Mitch did have to admit to himself that the warm liquid flowing through his insides made him feel more alive. He smirked at this thought: 'Or perhaps just a little less dead?' He looked around the dimly lit room. A typical native longhouse. Fire in the middle, smoke release in the roof center. It appeared to be almost Potawatomi in its construction, from what he had learned in engineering history class. Lots of birch bark. Much larger pieces than those from the battles, he noticed. The Brits must have brought them as far north as they had west.

If the Indian girl was telling him the truth, it was the first week of April. Still 1779, he seriously hoped.

The fire in the house was not small, but there was a chill in the air, nonetheless.

He broke the silence by baiting, as much as saying, "Why do you all speak such very good English for native Potawatomi?" He watched their faces for a reaction.

Gert looked at him and said, "Good guess, white man, but not quite right."

KT then interjected, "Captain, as I started to explain before, we are a confederacy now of four tribes. We have been forced into this confederacy over generations, mainly for protection. First by the long Iroquois wars, then Ottawa Chief Pontiac's Indian War against the British and British Colonials, and now by the British and yours."

She paused before she began to try to explain. "There are some Ojibwa, remnants of the Ottawa tribe, Potawatomi, Huron, and Wyandot here. The land this reservation is on, we call it Monguagon, named for this entire area, was most recently settled by the Wyandot.

"We are Wyandot and that is why the true warrior chief is Quay Quay, my and Gert's father. However, as we integrated, it was decided that we would be called the Huron Confederacy."

She continued the history/civics lesson: "Full-blooded Hurons are now few and far between, but the Wyandot have been amongst them for so long that we have merged in our manner of living and our tribal laws and customs."

Mitch interrupted, looking at Gert with a smile, "We revolutionaries should at least get partial credit for your new confederacy, right?" He winked at Gert.

Gert could not help but smile. "I will grant you that, white man, I will grant you that, but be careful what you form; it might just end you."

"Or maybe..." Mitch suggested, "create you?" He smiled again.

"Back to the subject." KT re-took control of the conversation. "The chiefs of the other tribes sit on the Elders Council and keep things running smoothly here, Captain Garrett, while my father helps the British." She wanted to add 'bastards,' but thought better of it.

"Only three of us," she swung her arm around the room indicating herself, Gert, and Jethro, "and our grandfather, the Great Chief Chewachta he is called, know of you and your...umm...condition. Oh, and you, of course," she said as an afterthought.

"Hell, you can't count me, seeing as I have no idea what condition I am in, aside from being dead and alive and apparently a little stronger than I was before I woke up.

"Oh, and another thing of a personal nature," he said loudly and strongly, so all in those in the longhouse could hear. KT braced herself.

"For the love of all that is holy, quit calling me captain. Never felt much like one when I was a live one, and I sure as blazes don't feel any more so being a dead one. You will please call me Mitch, just Mitch…understood?"

The face that looked so angry mere seconds ago softened before KT's eyes, and a small smile crossed his face.

The three nodded in understanding and let out a long-held, collective breath.

"Now that I have the local politics understood, can you answer my original question? How do all three of you talk such perfect English? Heck, KT, yours is better than mine."

"There are certain benefits to being the children and consort of the True Chief. When the English missionaries came to tell us of their sky god, they taught English to the select few. We went five days a week for many years during the winter months. Father insisted."

"Commanded is more like it," Gert added with a certain amount of bitterness.

"Gert never really enjoyed the classes, as I think you can guess," KT said.

"And you, Jethro?" asked Mitch, looking toward the very large man in the doorway. "Did you enjoy school?"

"It was warm, and they fed us at midday; that was good enough for me," he said with a big smile, which became contagious.

KT went on, "I also had the pleasure of spending three summers by the big river in Saint Clarice learning French from the strange men in black dress. You must have seen them; the ones they called Pre'tre or Cure' or Father or Padre, yet they did not seem very interested in having women or children of their own."

She stole a quick glance at Mitch to see if he had caught the sarcasm. He was already looking at her and smiling. He gave her a wink, as well, and went back to his bitter soup.

KT smiled inside and thought, 'You know what? This could turn out to be fun in a way; well, at least as much fun as the undead and vengeance can be.'

"Do you perhaps have any bitter bread and bitter butter to go with this lovely bitter soup?" Mitch asked, dripping of the sarcasm KT had assumed he had.

"Bread, yes, and I am glad you seem to have an appetite of any kind, but if you call me Betty, I will not be pleased." She smiled directly into his eyes. "And I don't sell seashells by the seashore, either, capt…I mean Mitch."

While Mitch and KT chuckled and relaxed at the shared joke, Gert and Jethro looked at each other with confusion, but not enough interest to ask.

As far as Gert was concerned, too much talking had already been done this day.

KT enjoyed the levity while it lasted but knew a much more important conversation was to come, and hopefully this seemingly good-natured Mitch would be able to come to terms with it, and more… much, much more.

Chapter Eight

The rest of the first day Mitch rested and ate assorted items presented to him.

He couldn't believe that he needed rest after a three-week nap, but he tired easily, and it helped keep him from just asking endless questions.

He was given a mirror to see himself for the first time since he had awakened.

His facial hair was exactly as it had been the morning of the battle. He wiped a bit of dirt from his chin, and he looked ready to fall in line and lead men into battle. The Oniaten inside him was finally able to see himself in this new form, and thought, 'Well, hell, this isn't so bad; a twenty-ish-year-old soldier with dark hair and quite a bit of muscle. Could have been a lot worse.'

Much to Mitch's surprise, he had heard the voice and looked desperately around him for some person he had not noticed. Seeing no one, he asked his mind, 'Who said that?'

'Oh, sorry about that,' the voice said, 'I didn't know you could hear me yet. I am the spirit inside you they have alluded to. I am the Oniaten.' Mitch continued listening, intrigued more than shocked.

'You are going to be told by these three what they think the powers of the Oniaten are. I will be listening and correcting, as necessary. Don't let them know you can hear me yet. I am curious how far off they are going to be. Plus, it will be interesting to see how they react when you start correcting them or finish their sentences. I would love some entertainment after all these years of quiet.'

Mitch knew it was not normal to hear voices in one's head, but normal wasn't in great supply at the moment, so he followed its advice.

'Just listen and don't appear threatening to them. They brought me back; they probably also have the ability to end me, and that means no more Mitch, too.' Mitch physically nodded as these words made sense in a slightly more normal way. The source was still a bit unsettling.

Mitch sensed the current conversation was over and began to think along the lines of more human amenities. To be honest, he was not very comfortable in his uniform anymore, though he was perplexed by the absence of his boots. He would have to ask about that.

Jethro was the only one in the longhouse with him at that time.

Mitch asked him, "Are there more comfortable clothes I might wear? This uniform is getting a bit uncomfortable after all these days and seems to have a very odd smell about it."

Jethro nodded as if expecting, perhaps hoping, for the question and pointed to a pile of clothes laying on the table across the room.

"KT figured you might ask. We have moccasins for you, too. As soon as we find out who swiped your boots, they will be returned," he said, as if reading Mitch's thoughts. "That smell you smell is the smell of death; you will smell it again!"

'Well, that sounded about as upbeat as everything else I've heard,' Mitch thought. He couldn't help but try to ask a few questions of the large man, the "chief's consort."

Jethro, obviously under strict orders, just kept repeating: "All will be explained the next day when the Great Chief Chewachta could be present and not arouse suspicions among the reservation."

"Even more a worry were the Brit guards and the prisoners in the pen. The same pen captured colonials and their allies are in." he concluded.

Then a deep, almost pained expression crossed the big man's face and he said, "There are some men of my own blood in that pen out there, and I can't blame them for fighting with the colonials, the Revolutionary Army I guess you are now." Only Mitch and the Oniaten were there to hear.

'The white men. Any of them at this point couldn't seem to be trusted to keep a promise anyway,' Jethro thought, getting angrier with each memory.

"Things have to change. Will change," he whispered, not loud enough for Mitch to hear him, but it was very loud to the old one within him.

Jethro looked over to see Mitch staring right at him, with a knowing, almost soul-searing smile and slightly nodded his head when their eyes met.

Jethro looked away quickly and went back to dutifully watching the opening to the longhouse.

Mitch laid down again and rested. 'Dead to the world,' he thought as his mind and thoughts went black.

The bright light from the opening of the door woke Mitch, as much as the draft that came with it.

Mitch's thoughts cleared almost immediately, much to his surprise. He thought to himself, 'Time to get up, Mitch Garrett. This is the second day of the rest of your life…or is it your death?'

One thing he could safely say out loud to himself was, "It should be a hell of a ride!"

Philosophy had never been his strong suit, and behind his seeming prediction of excitement and fun he had a sinking feeling that would have to change, and very soon at that!

The light from the opening of the longhouse was broken three times, as three must have entered, Mitch surmised.

The sudden light had rendered him virtually blind for the moment, then KT came next to him, touched his shoulder, and looked toward the others who had entered.

Just as his eyes started to clear, Jethro exited, causing the effect again, and Mitch was starting to think they were doing it on purpose now.

A couple of minutes passed, without further blindness.

Mitch noted that besides himself were KT, Gert, and what had to be the Great Chief Chewachta he had been told of. 'I'd call him Gramps if I was KT or Gert,' Mitch thought. He stifled the snicker, which the situation obviously did not call for.

He remembered he had cracked a few jokes at his parents' memorial and still had at their gravesides since. Those present at the time who heard these missives, their facial expressions, and body language seemed to suggest they thought him something almost demonic, in retrospect. Mitch smiled, thinking, 'Guess I got the last laugh there.' Each handles grief in their own way, and in his current state, he found some degree of humor in both his alive and his dead side.

'Fuck philosophy.' Mitch shook his head to clear it. 'I'm pretty sure I am gonna have to work harder on sanity.'

The great chief was brightly adorned with a headdress that was beyond description, but if Mitch had had to hazard one, it looked a little like a pheasant and a quail were trying to hide underneath an abnormally tall, round hat with a wide brim but couldn't seem to get all the feathers tucked in.

From across the battlefield, he remembered the head covering of Chief Quay Quay was worn much closer to his head and was of another shape entirely. He would have to ask KT about its significance at a better time.

'He is wearing the headdress of the eldest chief of this clan, show respect, but remember the true warrior chief is not here.

'Also,' the Oniaten added hastily, 'don't react out loud or in any physical way to what I am telling you unless I tell you to. Understood?'

"Yes," Mitch said out loud and immediately apologized in his head, saying, 'yep, my mistake; won't do it again if I can remember not to."

The Oniaten knew this to be true and just said, 'Good, talk with me in your head, or they will think you're insane and remove you from your current animated self and end me again at the same time.'

The others in the room noticed when he said the word out loud, but Chewachta waved off any thought of commentary on the outburst, or what it was in answer to.

By the light of the fire, Mitch jokingly estimated the great chief's age to be somewhere between 125 and 350. But the great chief sat down in front of the fire with seeming fluidity.

He crossed his legs and gazed into the fire.

Everyone else's eyes, including Mitch's, were on the great chief.

Mitch had to admit that the silence was a very effective tool. He was getting a little frightened by its duration.

No, he conceded, he was getting more terrified of it by the moment.

The Oniaten in his head said, 'Shut up, quit worrying, and pay attention!' Mitch felt he was in no position to argue the point and settled down.

KT motioned those who remained standing to sit. She then went and brought water to each, just setting the great chief's in front of him, as he still had not spoken.

'At least out loud or to us,' Mitch thought.

Chapter Nine

After what seemed like an eternity but was probably only about a 'hundred' years, Mitch postulated. Time at this point had lost relevance to him as he came to grips with what he was being told from inside and out.

He took a drink from the cup presented him after Gert and KT had. Water was still quite cool. It had only been a few minutes, he knew, but he wasn't sure if at this point he wanted the silence to end or continue. 'Better the devil, you know…?'

Suddenly, yet slowly, if such a thing is possible, the great chief lifted his head and methodically considered the faces of the three present, stopping at Mitch's last.

A stare that could bore a hole in a centuries old black hickory was now tunneling its way through Mitch's head; he could almost swear he could feel the heat. He stared right back at him with determination, and not to mention, a decided lack of a better plan.

In a voice so deep it rattled the wooden roof supports but no louder than a whisper, the old man said, "It is my honor to meet you, Captain Mitchell Garrett." And holding up his hand to stop any protest said, "And I understand you wish to be called Mitch. I will refer to you as such from this point forward.

"However, many will call you much different and, perhaps, worse things than that. I would advise you to toughen up your hide a bit."

Mitch, who had tensed at the full title, relaxed a little.

The silence broken, the fear he had felt dissipated into something closer to anxiety and more damn questions.

'Ya' know?' he thought. 'I really think I understand the R.I.P. on tombstones a lot better now.'

His attention was called back to the old chief as he continued rumbling, "I am sure you have been told some of what is happening. I am equally sure you think you do have a slight grasp on what is going on."

He looked at Mitch, then the others. "I am here to tell you what has really happened to you, what you have become, and the effects to expect. You will not believe me at first…if you did, you would be a fool and certainly never have become a captain if you were, for it will sound impossible to you.

"Hopefully in time, you will see it, feel it, come to terms with it, and then Mitch, what you do with it is up to you."

The Oniaten jumped into Mitch's mind and said, 'Don't worry; as long as you trust me, you will have a fine time of it.'

He stared at Mitch again; that same concentrated glare.

Mitch couldn't help but feel Chewachta was talking to, perhaps even hearing more than just Mitch the Revolutionary Captain at this point.

In fact, it seemed almost as if he were not talking to Captain Mitch at all.

'The strangest part,' thought Mitch, 'is that I know who the part of me he is talking to is and can hear him.' It was seeming to come back to Mitch's mind as an old memory does.

Only this was not his memory he was recalling, and the memory had little detail.

"A memory of a feeling, that's what it is," Mitch concluded, not realizing he had said it aloud.

The three others looked at him as one, and the old chief smiled, patted Mitch on the back gently, and said both kindly and simply, "Exactly, my friend, and it will serve you well if you can and-or will follow it."

The Revelation
Chapter Ten

"I think perhaps," the great chief said, "we should take some nourishment while we talk."

Then, turning to Mitch with genuine concern in his eyes, he said, "How is your appetite? Have you been able to eat?"

KT answered for him, "He takes some broth and bread but complains it tastes bitter."

"But I also said it felt good going down, and it does tend to warm me inside," Mitch qualified her answer.

"A little something right now actually sounds good; probably sounds better than it will taste." He shot a quick glance to KT and added, "To me, that is; I am sure your food is delicious. I meant no offense."

KT waved her hand in the air dismissively. "I told you I learned to read and write. Never said I learned to cook." Winking at him, she said, "Maybe, just maybe, it's not your taste after all."

KT brought out brown bread and dried meat; what type, Mitch didn't know and had learned enough at this point not to ask.

With their drinks refilled, Chewachta sat up straight and began a story, a story of long ago. In his younger days, words that Mitch hoped would soon shed extra light upon his current circumstances.

"When I was a young brave," Chewachta began, "if you can imagine that far back. Our people were settled along the big lakes to the north. Many tribes shared a vast area with each other and some scattered French trappers who wandered through from time to time, bartering with us, and buying extra furs from us.

"It was as I was approaching my adulthood that the new white men came from a land called England, the French told us. It was clear the French were no friends of the new settlers, advising us to verify everything they said, for they tended to be less than honorable when it came to any other than their own tribe."

He paused, looked off toward the opening in the roof, returned his eyes down, then said, "They came slowly at first and were respectful, for the most part. We allowed them to hunt on our lands and bartered with them as we had with the French." Chewachta continued, "Unlike the French, though, they started to build permanent settlements upon our lands.

"We had expected them to stay a season and move on, but like unwanted houseguests, they made themselves literally at home and rarely asked permission or gave any payment in return.

"We were patient at first, but they came in great numbers, cutting our available lands and starting to deprive us of the game we subsisted on."

The elder chief went on, "They made a treaty offer to the Iroquois tribe, who had accepted it, and agreed to move west for the price that was paid.

"That was all well and good for the Iroquois, but the countless other tribes in the area knew nothing of the deal and received none of the payment!" Chewachta's voice had gotten louder. He now seemed to notice that and continued, but in more subdued tones.

"When the settlers were told this, by our and other tribes, they refused to leave, make any further payments, or met our requests for them to leave, with guns.

"First there were the massacres in the night. Then stealing children, to be used as slaves, and taking our women for their own.

"After a brief struggle," he went on, "and with much bloodshed on both sides, we were forced to move west."

The chief looked up from his lap where his head had come to rest, staring straight ahead and said with a deep, almost palpable sadness, "I lost my mother during the trip. She was not old, but she had lived through much. I personally think it killed her to leave behind the land of countless generations of our brave and honorable men. To leave the bones of our ancestors behind. The sacred land to be dug up and cultivated or left as fallow fields to feed their domestic stock."

The silence returned for a moment. Mitch could swear he could hear everyone's heartbeat; well, except for his own, he thought morosely.

"This same thing happened over the course of the last fifty or more years; dozens of times, till we found ourselves out here on the fringes, near a whole other tribal land," said the elder chief, sounding angrier more than melancholy again now.

"We have literally been squeezed into this little area near our blessed river." He made wave motions with his hands now.

"I am sure it is but a matter of time before we shall be required to move again; where to from here?" He motioned around. "I cannot say."

"When we arrived here, we vowed that this would be the last stop on our westward journey and set about some way to ensure that. We were out-gunned, outnumbered, and outwitted; what did we have that they did not? What could we use that they could not defend against?"

The great chief looked at Gert and said, "So we began to resurrect the old powers; what your kind would call magic." He looked back at Mitch when he said the word "magic."

"We had a brilliant plan, did we not, Gert?"

Gert nodded his head strongly once but did not speak or look up at the chief.

"We decided we needed a warrior; one who could fend off the white man, and anyone else, for that matter. One who could form an army larger than all the white men on this great land combined."

"How could we do that, you might wonder Mitch?" the chief said, looking at him. "Here is the part you really need to pay attention to, for it now involves you."

'Well, this just gets better all the time!' Mitch thought despondently.

"You will remember the magic I spoke of?" the chief stated at, more than asked, Mitch.

"Yes, the one that would help you raise more men than your enemies could," Mitch replied.

"Well, that arrow was meant for my son, and not you…" Chewachta paused briefly before moving on. "The magic, or in this case, what some of your people might call poison, was on the arrowhead, and you took the full brunt of it, causing you to die. I think most of this you have contrived on your own?" He looked around the room for guilty faces and saw only agreement and continued concern.

The old chief continued, "I am equally sure you realize you are no longer what one would call dead, yet you have no heartbeat; therefore, not alive either, yes?"

Mitch nodded, waiting for the other shoe, maybe moccasin the better term, to drop.

"You are what in English would be called 'undead'."

"In our most ancient native tongue, you, and you alone, will be referred to as the Oniaten." Mitch heard him sound out the word, as the voice in his head echoed it: 'Oh-nee-otton.'"

"The name has remained the same for centuries, perhaps millennia, through most northern tribes, as you are the first to be formed in as many years."

"Gert here," he said, motioning toward the medicine man, "found some of the old writings and has been trying to put the magic together since he was just old enough to talk.

"It wasn't until we sent him away for proper schooling that he met white men who could help complete it. Of course, they had no idea what it was they were helping with. Gert had them convinced it was an elixir to strengthen manhood and promised a bottle to each man who helped along the way."

Everyone looked at Gert, who was smiling broadly.

"Nothing motivates them more. Especially the older ones!

"It is the whiskey of the white man," he completed his thought, still smiling.

The brief moment of levity gave Mitch a chance to think about what he had been told, which was essentially just what he already knew and a new name to be called Oh-nee-otton.

He would have to get the spelling from KT at a better time. He knew that the other moccasin was still very much in the air and apparently had reservations about making the drop. Mitch inwardly winced at the poor choice of the words in his head, and he felt a little anger at the word reservation…

"That being accomplished," the old man continued, "we waited for the right minute when we could be at our strongest.

"The Brits had started to trust us, especially my son, and then…well…you tried to be a hero and got yourself undead; that and a light finger on a bow string!"

Mitch shot a quick glance at Gert, who was no longer smiling.

"Now that the poison has done its bit, the magic will become stronger. You, Mitch, must be its equal, its master until it becomes you and you become it."

"An Oniaten," said Mitch with a certain finality to his tone. Then he asked, "Will I be recognized as such among your tribe? "Will I have to stay in this hut until…well…when? What kind of path, future do I have ahead of me?" His hands first motioning around the hut, then toward the door.

"You already look for the end to this story, and I have yet to begin to tell it to you," the chief said, shaking Mitch from his moment of confused anger.

"You will live in your current state forever." Even the elder chief seemed burdened having to utter that reality.

He spoke the words, trying not to sound like a clerk at the trading post having to explain to a customer that there had been a mix up at the feed store back home…then intoned…slightly menacingly. "The only way you can die is the same way you died last time.

"Know that we still possess that poison and will not hesitate to use it if you stray from the path the magic will lead you."

Mitch went gray but slowly nodded his head. Calmly, he said, "Understood, Chief Chewachta, very well understood."

"In addition, and this is where it starts to become a little more delicate, you must be very careful where you walk."

This time it was KT's voice that delivered the news. Looking up at her face from the firelight, he could see a glimpse of whimsy in her eyes, almost like an inside joke with his insides, but not with him…quite yet.

"Yes," Gert said, "I wouldn't visit your parents' burial grounds if I were you…unless you have a very important question…and a very strong stomach."

Inside Mitch's mind a clarification from the Oniaten: 'Mitch, you can visit your parents' grave anytime you want. Just don't have me ask them any questions, unless of course they are really important.'

Inside the Oniaten's portion of Mitch's mind was a feeling that this event was more likely than not to occur. Also, it was not the Oniaten's problem at this moment. 'Soon enough.' the ancient spirit mused.

This, Mitch noticed, was met with glares at Gert from the others, but it left Mitch with the desire to say something inappropriate. (We all handle grief differently, he remembered).

"Dad did say I was to have his pocket watch when he went. Wonder if he still has it with him?"

Now the other three looked at him in complete astonishment.

Even Jethro turned away from the door to look at him. "For as long as it took for the poison to wear off, it seems the magic is making up the lost time," Chewachta said with a satisfied grin.

The Oniaten, also taken with the calmness of his new "warrior," thought, 'This lad was born for this, whether he wanted to be or not.'

Chapter Eleven

It had been a long three days; tales of old, tales of new, tales of magic and of destiny.

Not mere tales Mitch was fully aware, but history already written and yet to be…at his hands it appeared.

More information and hopeful conjecture had been thrown at Mitch, the Oniaten, than even he had believed possible to digest.

He still felt empty and was left working without a map. Thankfully, the Oniaten was up to the task and explained, in a real way, what Mitch would be looking forward to.

"So, you mean to tell me?" Mitch more screeched than said to the gathered corporeal folks, paused and regrouped. Pacing in an ever-widening circle, he cleared his throat and said in a calm, normal voice to the room at large, "Let me see if I have this straight."

Every eye in the room was upon him.

He started again, smiling a slightly maniacal smile and looking from KT to the elder chief.

"I have, through little or no fault of my own, mind you, become a champion for your people. An undead doorman between the living world and that of the departed?"

KT looked to her grandfather with a bit of apprehension in her eyes. His eyes never met hers, but she saw in them something that calmed her.

"Charon of this, the new River Styx, perhaps?" Mitch continued, waving his hands in the direction of the river behind the longhouse.

He spun quickly toward KT and hissed, "I never missed a Greek history lesson."

He paused and took a deep breath, and the bizarre expression on his face reappeared. The strange smile was, in fact, a result of the Oniaten recognizing a hero when he was embodying one.

Reluctant as he might be, he…this low-self-esteem soldier, wanna-be engineer, would serve the cause well.

Turning back toward the chief, Mitch said, "And when exactly, Chief Chewachta, is this great new age clash to begin?"

Chewachta gazed at him, almost with a sense of awe. "In time, son, in time. The Oniaten inside you will know before any of us, even before you, Captain Mitchel Garett, I am afraid. Remember I told you it would be an adjustment."

The Oniaten confirmed to Mitch this was accurate and would be appropriate to respond to.

"Yes, you have told me a lot of things. I have no reason—yet—to doubt you, but somehow… strangely…I wish I did."

His voice trailed off as he sat heavily at the chair usually occupied by Jethro, who was currently seated outside the entrance.

Gert had been sitting in the far back of the house, listening quietly and holding a bow and arrow that Mitch could only imagine held the only release from his current condition. ('The green glow was a dead giveaway,' Mitch told himself, with a bit of ironic humor.) But…just…damn it, he had to admit he had already started to feel more comfortable and formidable with each passing hour, and he desperately wanted to see how it played out.

He smiled a genuine smile and looked up from his position toward the chief and KT and started to agree when a thumping at the entrance startled him, followed quickly by what was clearly a Brit: "Major Timmons to see Great Chief Chewachta!"

The Pen

Dieke sat on the fallen tree that was trying really hard to be a bench and looked across the muddy… corral…is what the men called it? The pen is what the redcoats called it.

To sum it up, it stood as a wet, muddy, sloppy shithole, with lean-tos as cover for a more-or-less steady late spring rain.

'Has it really been over a month since the bastards forced us here?' he thought to himself.

Dieke, having never been a religious man or from a religious family, thought, 'If the authors of the Bible were asking for my pick of a description of hell, this would certainly be on the short list.

'On the bright side,' he thought, 'I am the leader of this group of lost souls.'

That sounded a lot better than what he was actually doing, which was keeping these ruffians and fools from killing each other, trying to escape, being shot dead, or successfully escaping to become bear food.

The "Mukwa" was what the natives called the bear. They were the Mukwa clan and had a great, almost super-holy respect for the beast.

"I have to be in charge of this bloody mess cause Mitch had to go and get himself killed," Dieke bitterly expressed, feeling both the anger and the pain of losing a friend. No, not just a friend…a best friend in a battle they had lost anyway.

"Perhaps in a way," Dieke posited aloud, overlooking the muddy cage he was in, "he was the luckier one?"

He watched as the redcoats walked the perimeter of the pen, long guns always at the ready.

Even them, so mentally bored, looking for something or someone to do, or shoot. Dieke knew this to be a dangerous time, and before that thought had left his mind, the noise along the river road caught everyone's attention.

From the nearest links of the pen, Dieke watched a very long and slow procession of redcoats.

Muddied, some bleeding, some limping, others carried, all moving toward the main British wooden garrison opposite the river and the pen. It was just barely visible from the corral-like enclosure.

Johan Bunte sloshed over and sat next to Dieke. "Those limey bastards looked to be in pretty bad shape, sir; and did you see how many of them returned?" Dieke nodded and looked toward the British camp.

"Maybe the fight has started to turn?" Johan, or Jon as everyone called him, said with more optimism than Dieke had heard from a man since the trip here had begun.

"Perhaps…" Dieke spoke softly, almost to himself as much as Jon, "or maybe their replacements had shown up just after the battle. Hard to tell from here."

Dieke knew there were too many for it just to be replacements…Something was definitely happening, and the knowledge it was happening to them was reason enough for hope.

"Hopefully, our boys don't look just as bad," Dieke said out loud to Jon and, well, to the universe at large.

A brighter reality entered Dieke's mind as he realized they seemed to have brought no prisoners with them. What's more, no natives from either side. "Damn, maybe this thing is turning in our favor."

'For now, all it did was increase the number of guards available to keep an eye on us,' his rational mind said, talking him down from doing or saying something stupid.

"Maybe our boys are right on their heels, coming to set us free!" Jon said almost giddily.

Dieke highly doubted that but wasn't about to throw cold water on Jon's happiness.

"Maybe so, Jon, maybe so!" He said it with an attempted smile that he hoped looked real, all the while patting Jon on the back.

Dieke returned to his makeshift bench as at first slowly and then increasingly, his fellow prisoners came up to him to share their thoughts and to get his opinion on what might be happening on the battlefront to force so many of the enemy here. Here, to the middle of nowhere!

Dieke handled each response as he had with Jon; a weary and cautionary optimism but continually reminding them it would have little effect on them, at least for now.

Dieke, suspicious by nature in the best of times, also noticed that the gathering of men around the "bench" should have drawn some attention from their British guards.

Surveying the grounds, he noticed the British guards were also gathered together at the other end of the pen, talking and occasionally pointing toward the main encampment.

The native guards were gathering, as well, close to the main longhouse of Great Chief Chewachta and close to their own nightly quarters.

"Well, that pretty much settles it," he said aloud, but mostly to himself. "Something big indeed has happened!"

The Pen, Part II

Captive life continued its normal course throughout the next few days. However, just under the surface, all present could feel a sense of foreboding, mixed with the desperate, almost palpable desire for hope.

Dieke, yet again, surveyed the pen, as was his responsibility. Same thing every day.

The plenteousness of wild game and fish, combined with the cooking skill of their native captors, provided good, even nourishing meals. "Better," Dieke admitted to himself, "than the army had delivered."

Although he did miss the tents the army had provided. "Not sure we'll survive long without more than these lean-tos to protect us."

Dieke knew they had been moved north as much as west, and these winters would likely be worse than those of New York, much less Pennsylvania.

"Let's hope we have better lodging; better yet, let's hope we are all home before the snow flies!"

Dieke noticed a red-coated officer come through the pen's main gate and advance to the great chief's longhouse, with regulars at either side, looking menacingly at the revolutionary soldiers ambling along their path.

Dieke was watching intently now. They stopped in front of the longhouse and one of the escorts announced loudly, "Major Timmons to see Great Chief Chewachta."

After what seemed to Dieke an inordinate amount of time, certainly long enough to annoy the British contingent at the door, the flap folded back, and after a few more words, they were allowed inside.

'Well,' Dieke thought, 'something big *is* happening; hope someone lets me know what it is before these men start making their own wild guesses. Nothing is harder to control than a bunch of desperate men with fantasies in their heads.'

The Pen, Part III

"I'll be damned," Dieke said loudly, standing by the fence of the enclosure and watching three rows of bright red uniforms march off to the east, down the river road. "The bloody redcoats are leaving. Hell, looks like all of them, too!"

This brought a thunderous cheer from the men surrounding him enjoying the sight of the British withdrawal.

'What, pray-tell, will they do with us now?' Dieke reflected silently, a very dark thought crossing his fertile imagination.

Two days later, Dieke's fears manifested.

Left without any British direction, the natives, who seemingly all had a wholly different vision of the prisoners present and future, met. Some wished to make them slaves, some to free them and see who could survive the swamps and ague of the area. Some wished, as Chewachta, that they could work together to improve the general area since it seemed the British currency and goods would no longer flow to this place.

Dieke, always mandatorily present as any negotiations took place, listened with feigned interest. The native prison guards and his own people in a circle around the "bench," were in attendance.

He was, himself, thinking about how to just escape this entire mess but remembered something from this awful nightmare.

During a lapse in negotiations about latrine duty and broth dispersal, he interrupted Great Chief Chewachta's monologue and simply asked, "Great Chief, where is your son, the true war chief of this Wyandot nation?"

Dieke remembering whose side the chief had been on…or so he thought. "Qua Qua, I believe?" He deliberately mispronounced the words he had heard dozens of times.

An outside observer noticed the reaction of everyone near Dieke. Especially those of the medicine man, grandson of the great chief and son of…

"Quay Quay," Gert corrected loudly to all present, never being far from the chief's side. He stood and faced the soldier, a clear challenge to those watching.

Dieke, however, never the first to pick up on physical cues, merely looked at the great chief and Gert's reactions with genuine curiosity.

In what seemed like no time to the observer, a nearby native warrior guard grabbed what could best be described as a red club, obviously intent to avenge the dishonor of Warrior Chief Quay Quay and release its impact on the soldier.

Unexpectedly, the medicine man, Gert, moved to defend the soldier and took the brunt of the force to his forehead, falling immediately at his grandfather's feet.

'The darkness, the beautiful darkness!' Gert, or what had been Gert, thought as he saw life from the other side. Slowly, though, the darkness started to take shape.

First a light in the middle. Then colors. Then trees. Then a great river. Deer appeared in front of him as the scope of this vision expanded to fill his eyes and his mind. Gert's joy was overwhelming; he had never felt so alive in his whole existence. The light from this sun was warm; warm but not hot. Wildlife was everywhere. "What an amazing place!" he screamed. His scream echoed off the nearby bluffs, and with their dying echoes, the fringes of this beautiful visage faded. First from the edges, then even the middle had darkened to black again.

A closer inspection of the darkness revealed a small light in what had to be at a distance, as it appeared to grow larger as it approached. The light came close to him now, to the injury to his head, it seemed. He felt no pain, but a sincere loss at being so close to a paradise he was being taken from. It was then a face formed within his still possibly indistinct vision.

An ancient native face stared into his, and he immediately knew it to be the Oniaten, and he was saying something... "Can't have you leaving us yet, young man. We need a medicine man for what comes next!"

Seeing the sadness left behind in Gert's face, the spirit said, "I know, lad... I know. I have seen it, too."

Gert, if questioned years later, would have sworn he saw a tear in the Oniaten's eye.

"Gert...no!" came a scream that everyone in the camp recognized as KT's as she ran out of the longhouse, apparently alerted to the tragedy as it happened.

The next thing Gert remembered was seeing Mitch's face where the Oniaten's had just been asking him something...what was it? What was he asking?

"Who am I?"

"Mitch, are you okay?" he whispered. "It's me, Gert."

Dieke watched KT run toward the scene, toward him, almost in slow motion, running to see to her brother, who was obviously badly hurt, a wound intended for him. Then someone else caught his attention.

A very pale man in native garb ran out from the longhouse behind her, and at an amazing speed, he caught and passed her on the run. He leaned over the badly bleeding man. The newcomer grabbed him by the head and held it to this breast. Dieke watched as the man's last breaths left his body; watched as the pale man continued to hold his head.

Words were not spoken but nonetheless filled seemingly every space available.

The medicine man, whose face was hidden from Dieke, who was a yard or so away, began to move, first his arms, then legs. He heard him whisper his name, "Gert."

When the pale man moved out of his view, he could see the man had neither scratch nor damage and was very much alive. KT held both the pale one and her brother and gently kissed both.

Then she said to her recovering brother, "Well, I guess he," then looking at both finished, "is your responsibility now."

Dieke, who at this point would be hard pressed to see something that shocked him, waited and watched as the pale man turned toward him and said, "Hey, Dieke, thanks for filling in for me. I have been a bit busy!"

Chapter Twelve

Somewhere between a triad of hate, relief, and amazement, Dieke looked into Mitch's eyes.

Very different eyes, he noticed, both in color and intensity.

'Mitch Garrett, the son of a bitch who died and should still remain on that battlefield. Mitch Garrett who had gone and left him to care for these ungovernable prisoners, and for what?' Dieke raged in his mind. 'He was warm and safe in that longhouse this whole time?'

It was only a second or two before he also realized Mitch just brought a man back from the dead after apparently returning from the dead himself.

"I bloody knew something wasn't right," he said aloud as he was finally directed to follow the newly reanimated Mitch and the even more recently reanimated Gert into the longhouse.

They left an entire company of men, both friend and foe, both native and colonial, to stand in the pen with no answers, but more questions than they had ever had…combined.

Before anyone had gone far into the investigation, a native warrior came to the flap that served as a door. He spoke to Jethro, then Gert in a language Mitch shouldn't have been able to understand, but somehow did.

Mitch paused as the rest went further into the structure, as did Chewachta and Dieke.

What Mitch heard from this warrior's report let him know quite quickly what the next days would require.

The native saluted the great chief and the medicine man Gert while backing out of the roundhouse.

Great Chief Chewachta motioned for Dieke to sit down on the rough-hewn log bench, close to the entrance.

The rest went further into the recesses of the gloom. Dieke sat and saw movement from the back of the roundhouse. He could just make out Mitch, KT, and Gert, who still seemed to be in fine shape, against all the evidence he had just witnessed. "Is this some game, some trick?" he shouted.

Then from the back came Mitch's voice: "No games and no tricks, my good friend, but one hell of a story. Unfortunately, most of it is yet to be written."

"Good news?" Mitch said, coming ever closer and into some light. "You're one of the main characters. Bad news? It might get you killed. Then again you were a revolutionary soldier, so you expected that…right?"

Dieke jumped out of his chair and headed across the floor, toward Mitch.

Chewachta, Gert, and KT came seemingly out of nowhere to cut him off. Clutching him by the chest, KT whispered into his ear, "Bad idea" as she directed him, quite forcefully, even perhaps, hopefully, sensually, Dieke thought, (but he had been away from brothels for a while, so his definition of sensual was a bit skewed), to a seat at the table.

He took the hint and sat.

Mitch slowly came out of the remaining shadow, stood over Dieke, leaned down, and looked again into the eyes of his once dear friend.

"Dieke, I need you to please ask as few questions as you can and to please trust me and these wonderful people." He motioned to the living and the undead alike.

Chapter Thirteen

Mitch, Dieke, KT, Gert, and Great Chief Chewachta all sat at the table in the middle of the longhouse.

The silence was deafening, and the looks ranged from hatred to confusion to a single thousand-mile stare, Dieke had heard it called, emanating from Mitch.

Great Chief Chewachta spoke first. "Captain Carson, much of what you are about to hear…"

Dieke cut him off by saying, "Oh, no, Lieutenant Carson, Captain Garrett sits right here. I am no longer captain of anything!"

Chewachta looked at Mitch and said, "What is it with you colonials and refusing ranks?"

Mitch's stare re-entered the room, and he looked at Dieke. "Sorry, mate, battlefield promotion…but, hey, think of the increased pension."

The attempted joke did exactly what Mitch hoped it would; it made everyone very uncomfortable and Dieke just a little angrier.

Dieke rose in obvious fury. Mitch slammed his fist into the table, causing it to not so much splinter but disintegrate under his fist. He said so quietly you had to feel it more than hear it, "Captain Carson, sit down *now*. I may no longer outrank you, but I have seniority, and no matter how much you piss me off, you are a soldier of the Revolutionary Colonial Army and will behave as such."

Dieke acquiesced to the request, more or less, in his mind.

What he actually did was stare in amazement at the pile of sawdust that was once a hundred-year-old table, made of trees many hundreds of years older than that. He looked up at Mitch, who was smiling, slightly maniacally at him and felt a little sick to his stomach.

No longer in the mood to argue about anything, he simply whispered, "Yes, sir."

"As I was saying, *Captain* Carson," Chewachta continued, "what you are about to hear will have less impact on you now…" He motioned around the floor, indicating the table event. He shot a disapproving glance at Mitch, who replied with a smile that if it could talk would say, 'You're welcome is going to sound a little less unbelievable.'

Over the next hour, Chewachta, KT, the undead Gert, and occasionally Mitch explained what had happened and what Mitch now was and represented.

Dieke's emotions, while listening, ranged from hate to sadness to vengeance, but the overwhelming one continued to be insanity. 'I never thought of insanity as an emotion before,' reflected Dieke as his mind reeled, and yet the words kept coming.

"When the redcoats left, they asked us to keep you and your soldiers prisoner until their eventual return." Chewachta continued, "We refused!"

Dieke's face softened a bit. "They, of course, were not happy with our answer, and in response, they said they would keep my son, Chief Quay Quay. You do remember him, yes?" The Great Chief looked at Dieke and instantly saw that he did and the mixed feelings he had for him.

"The messenger has told us the remaining redcoat forces in this area are gathering at the shallows, where this river," he motioned to where the river ran outside the longhouse, "meets the great river and the shallows, where they will depart. Surrender, if you will, and return to British North America, to Fort Malden on the other side of the big water."

He continued without so much as a breath, and a rising anger, They intend to take Quay Quay with them; a hostage to force us to serve them!"

Dieke felt the old man's anger, similar to his own…and he felt something else, too; the rising body heat of the man sitting next to him, his friend, his compatriot and something else, too…Mitch.

Now Mitch stood, patted the old chief on the shoulder, and motioned toward a chair at what was once a table.

Gert and KT stared at him. 'As if this was something new,' thought Dieke.

"Dieke," Mitch softly spoke, "we would very much like for you and, well, I guess one must say, my revolutionary detachment, to help these people get their chief back. In return, they, and once again I guess I have to say, or perhaps should say, we, will make sure you capture and kill enough of the blimey bastards to keep them from ever interfering with the colonies' activities in this area *ever*." (Mitch said this much louder than was necessary, but he was starting to get the hang of dramatic effect after the table thing).

"And…" he added, whispering in Dieke's ear, "if you think this is strange for you, walk a mile in my moccasins and my military boots."

Dieke looked from the living to undead to a living face and saw the same thing from each. "We would really like you to help us, but this is going to happen with or without you."

"Well, say I can get them to agree with it? What in the hell I am supposed to tell them about what they have seen with the big guy here?" Dieke motioned to Gert.

"What I would tell them is we are going to go kick some British ass, and these people are going to help us if we help them.

"You will see things you have never seen before, but you will have a victory no one has ever had before. You can be heroes in this land and a friend of the natives you must live near if you wish to live in peace in this new nation," Mitch said.

"Now, what you should tell them is were going to go kick some redcoats off our land and the natives are going to help us and let everyone's memory be left to them to interpret," Mitch said with finality.

Chewachta started, "They start to leave almost immediately from what we have gathered, so we need an answer from you—"

"Have our men prepared by morning, Dieke!' Mitch interrupted. "I will start to raise the native army at dusk tomorrow evening. We need the living to have their shit together before Gert and I leave for the shallows tomorrow, no more than two hours before dusk."

He stated without possibility of correction, for the Oniaten had shown him a glimpse, from his previous incarnation, what lay before them. Mitch would be more worried if he did not know he could command a vast army of the dead (Gert's death/rebirth had shown him that.) that would help drive off the red-coated bastards, stealing KT's earlier thought.

The words came from Mitch's mouth, but they weren't his, nor were they in his voice and they 'might not even have been in English,' Dieke would think years later when retelling this story to his grandchildren.

Dieke looked up at what was at least partially his old friend and said, "I will gather them and tell them, but I must tell them they will be free after this…and be able to back it up!" Dieke was ever smelling something foul in what seemed quite straight forward.

"You may tell them they are free now, if you wish, but if they are the men I fought beside and led, the chance to kill a lot of enemy soldiers should entice them to battle," Mitch, 'the real Mitch,' Dieke thought, said.

Mitch walked away, leaving Dieke to himself to think about how best to relay this information to his men and secretly hoping most of them would remain.

Dieke was shaken from his thought when the native princess, KT, approached him.

He gazed at her, what in retrospect would probably have been considered more of a leer. She was quite beautiful, and he had watched her around the camp, even spoken with her a few times as she provided the meals to the then-prisoners. She motioned toward the seat facing him and asked, "Do you mind if I sit with you?"

He stood immediately and held the chair, for lack of a better term, for her while she adjusted to the small table between them.

"We have not officially been introduced, but you should call me KT. I am to understand you are Captain Dieke Carson?"

"Just Dieke, Dieke will be fine. A great pleasure it is to know the princess of the reservation, and one hell of a cook, if you don't mind me sayin'."

KT visibly blushed and turned away. "Please, just think of me as one of the tribe. I'm really not interested in the princess stuff; that is more a European title. I consider myself one, small part of this large community we have built and this war has almost destroyed."

She looked to Dieke for a reaction, but he just stared at her, either ignoring her or digesting every word, she wasn't quite sure which.

She continued nonetheless, "I do so hope your men will help us rescue my father. I would consider it a personal favor if you were to lead your men into this battle."

Dieke felt her hand grab his left leg, just above the knee and squeeze as she said, "A personal favor."

'I might be getting the hang of these physical cues after all,' he thought.

He leaned across the table, and she matched his motion, their faces mere inches apart. Dieke whispered, "For you, my princess, I would fight the whole British army by myself." He smiled, touched her chin, brought her head up to meet his, then kissed her on the forehead.

KT's reaction was one of relief and frustration. She really liked this man, and she knew he felt the same, but there will be time for more when he returns. As an afterthought of that feeling, she said to him, "You promise me you will come back?" She attempted to smile demurely, not quite sure she had pulled it off, and continued, "I think I would really like to know you better."

"You can count on it, princess. I would also like to know everything about you." He winked at the end of the statement, and KT blushed again, grabbed his hand from the table, kissed the back of it, and said, "Please, come see me before you leave tomorrow. I just might have something for you."

She got up and walked away, with Dieke noticing her hips swaying as she did so, his mind reeling at what she might have for him the next day. The possibilities at this point seemed endless.

Chapter Fourteen

The conclaves were held by Dieke and the colonials, with a special appearance from Captain Garrett to verify the native's offer and also, by Chewachta and the remaining Wyandot nation, with a special appearance from the Oniaten to verify the colonial's answer.

At noon the next day, all members of the compound in its current state met in what had been the pen, dismantled by colonials and natives, side by side.

Emerging from inside of the chief's longhouse, with the door held open by Jethro, came Great Chief Chewachta, followed by Mitch, then Gert, and eventually KT.

Chewachta and Mitch took the center in front of the assembled motley mass of soldiers and warriors.

KT noticed that a few of the native warriors she now saw she knew to have died in the last year. KeeTawa, the brother of one of her friends, had died of ague less than a month ago; she had attended the burial. His and the others eyes glowed to her, but if any of the other warriors noticed or cared, she saw no indication.

Chewachta was the first to speak: "The Mukwa clan honor those of you white men who have chosen to stay and help us." He held up a hand to quiet the expected complaints that it was, in fact, the natives who were helping the revolutionary force.

"We, in exchange, hope you honor us who are willing to help you defeat these men who would dishonor both of our peoples!"

Mitch had started it, but by the end, battle cries of every nature were echoing off the trees, the river, the longhouse, the roundhouses, and what was left of the British barracks.

KT again noticed that the new warriors joined in as much as was possible. Gert and Mitch could be heard above the rest and seemed to shake the ground, scattering the local fowl, the local wildlife, and more than a few corpses that were buried close enough to hear the Oniaten when he spoke loudly enough.

She had to admit the white men were reserved in their shock at half-mangled and decomposing natives who came to full attention and lined up at Mitch's yell.

Now it was Mitch's turn to speak. Dieke watched, wondering how much of a spectacle this might become. As Mitch began to speak, all eyes were on him. Even nature seemed to pause so he could be heard. Two, distinct sets of eyes now watched him from the forest, unseen by any, except, perhaps, each other and the Oniaten himself.

How it could best be described by an outsider: Mitch spoke in not just English, and not just the native language, but translated into every language spoken in the area; hell, maybe on the entire planet. To each listener, he was talking just to them, and they couldn't not hear it, even if they had been born deaf or without ears.

"Tonight, my warriors, we seek two goals, two independent goals, but they are not exclusive; they are tied together. We have never before been more brothers!"

The assembled armies eyed each other, not with suspicion or anger, but with a soldier's sense of who would be good at what when the battle began.

Mitch noticed the unification as if it were a wave; illusionary walls falling, prejudices set aside by one common mission.

"Destroy the oppressors! Save the chief!" Mitch and the Oniaten said as one, and 'for the very first time,' KT thought. That thought alone gave her shivers.

She had been an observer since Gert had become reanimated.

Gert now, it had been determined, could not go more than three hundred paces from Mitch without returning to being dead, so he took over her duties.

It had left her melancholy, but she knew it also made a much stronger war party.

The Oniaten was alongside the medicine man who had created him, and who could, if need be, end him.

'A match made in hell,' she thought, remembering the words of the nuns of the French settlers in Detroit and Saint Clarice.

"Gert and I," Mitch motioned toward Gert, "will leave at five hours past high noon, down the river road, toward the British disembarking point." His further instructions included that the current force at the reservation would leave exactly forty-five minutes after, giving the Oniaten time to 'rouse' the troops along the way, so that by the time they were past the Monguagon lowlands, they would be in force, and the entire company of resistance could meet at once.

Thankfully, the quick, unexpected, and forced retreat of the redcoats had left many weapons and a store of ammunition behind.

Dieke was busy making sure his soldiers had everything they needed to go into battle, including an extra preloaded musket each.

A large meal of wild game, fish, and everything available was prepared for the soon-to-be departing armies. Small amounts of alcohol were dispersed to fortify the troops for what they were about to endure, some would say. For what they were about to see, others might say.

KT, seizing the moment of calm, caught Dieke's eye and motioned him over to the back side of the longhouse. When he was close enough, she grabbed his hand and led him down, closer to the river.

"The nuns," she said, "believed this to have magic powers of protection. They gave it to me, hoping I would believe in and trust their god."

She continued, "I never did and don't find it likely that I ever will, but I know your people believe in that same god, so if there is any magic in it, I want you to have it."

She reached out her hand and held a golden cross on a rough chain. "Please take this and promise me you will return it to me yourself."

Dieke considered her face and noticed the tears forming her eyes. He grabbed both her hands, took the cross and chain from her, and leaned in and kissed her deeply. More deeply, emotionally, than either had ever kissed or been kissed before, they would later tell their grandchildren, much to the children's comically dramatized disgust.

"I promise you, my princess, I will return this to you as soon as I can, and maybe I'll have a little something more for you when I return." This time he did not wink but looked her deeply in the eyes and gently kissed her lips again.

He backed away slightly. "And I wouldn't worry with Mitch around. I don't think much damage can be done to any of us…well, any that hasn't already been done."

He smiled a wry smile, bowed slightly, and left KT staring…okay, leering after him. She noticed his hips sway as he walked away, and she smiled a deep smile, leaned against the wall of the longhouse, and let out a long sigh.

Elrich

(Meanwhile, some forty-five miles to the north)

"All I am saying is Kent told me that during his flight last night, at least three new ladies had arrived at the French town," explained the tall, dishwater blonde vampyre everyone just called Sandy.

The three vampyres at the table were several pints into a good day of drinking.

"Well, I know where I am heading this evening," said Elrich, whom the other vampyres made a habit of making fun of his dyed, blonde, spiked hair.

"I could use some new 'blood,' if you'll pardon the pun."

The other two vampyres rolled their eyes so hard it almost made an audible noise.

"You have got to get some new material," said Gavin. "That joke is older than the three of us combined."

Gavin was almost a perfect cross between the other two vampyres, except for his long brown hair, but with a fair complexion, almost as pale as Elrich, but taller than him and shorter than Sandy.

To the casual observers sitting throughout the tavern in the big city the priests had named Saint Clarice, the three men looked like ordinary people in their mid-twenties, out for a good time. All would be shocked to learn they were vampyres; the youngest, Gavin, was 167 years old. They all spoke with different accents, if listened to closely enough, but every one of them in perfect English.

Elrich was the oldest of the three present vampyres at 215 years. Sandy was a mere 181.

About halfway through their next pint, Kent arrived.

A pint was brought to the table before he even arrived at his seat. The bar maid, Daphne, who placed the pint down as he arrived, smiled at him.

Kent said, "I thank thee, my lovely," and leaned down and gently kissed her on her cheek. She blushed and looked away, but anyone watching could tell she was quite smitten with the attractive man.

Kent sat. He had short, black hair slicked back and had a very heavy British accent, which was just one of the reasons Daphne and, well, frankly most of the single female population of Saint Clarice, found him irresistible. (Possibly more than singles, or females).

He greeted the others.

His appearance was strikingly muscular, adding, of course, to his attractiveness in every way.

Rumor had spread that a Mukwa (Native Spirit Bear) would not even choose to fight him. Considering his true nature, there would be no question he believed.

"Finally!" It was Elrich who first spoke as the others nodded to Kent's arrival. "Tell me every detail about the new girls you saw!"

Elrich stared into Kent's eyes to make sure he got all the details right. "Well, I went south for my nightly flight," Kent began. "I roosted in the peak of the boarding house, the main one, when a fancy coach arrived."

"Yeah, yeah, fancy coach and all; who cares about that! What about the girls?" Elrich more-or-less yelled.

Kent smiled, and knowing a captive audience when he saw one, said, "I'm getting to that.

"The very black coach came to a halt in front of the house. The coachman climbed down, opened the door, and bowed deeply." He paused for effect as he began to pantomime the scene.

"Down the steps came an amazingly beautiful creature with long, black hair, darker features, and wearing an elegant gown; you know, the kind royalty wears, right?"

The others nodded, somehow feeling, in a strange way, that no one would wear that for a trip of this kind, unless it was a hurried one.

"The beautiful one," Kent continued, "spoke to the coachman in a language I barely understood, then he rose and backed away."

'Royalty of some sort beyond doubt,' Elrich said to himself.

"You said there were three!" he interrupted, echoed by a smiling Sandy.

"Patience, patience lads. I'm getting to them."

Kent continued, "Behind her were two, very pale girls, with long hair, reddish blonde, probably twins. They were dressed nicely, but nowhere near the fanciness of the dark lady. They never spoke, only stared straight ahead. They followed the lady in virtual lockstep into the boarding house.

"I followed the coach, which was taken to the livery and released from its horses. It appears, my comrades, the girls plan to be here awhile," Kent concluded.

Chapter Fifteen

At five hours past high noon, give or take, Mitch and Gert loaded three horses with general supplies.

"You are sure you know where all these graves are, right?" Mitch asked Gert.

"I know the ones I have heard of; there are probably more from many generations earlier. They will also respond, Mitch. We will have a force, I promise."

The Oniaten let Mitch know Gert was correct and that he had given his call to all warriors, or even want-to-be warriors past and present, then considered the future, but thought that was to be saved for another day.

"Never doubted you for a minute, Gert and, hey, remember to stay close!" Mitch said, winking with a level of humor Gert seemed to not appreciate.

The assembled army, led by agreement, by Captain Dieke Carson, stood and watched as the two of them and their three horses started to slowly ride the still-muddy river road, prepared to move in forty-five minutes exactly.

The intermittent heavy rain since the British withdrawal had not made preparing for battle any easier, but 'it was never going to be easy anyway,' Mitch thought.

Mitch's horse didn't seem very comfortable with an undead rider. Gert's wasn't terribly thrilled with the idea, either, but neither gave the men much trouble.

They made it past the turn and out of the view of the camp. Several of the new native warriors, the ones KT had noticed, were coming along, whether they were asked or not.

Mitch and Gert knew why and paid no attention, other than to note they now had a rear guard they had not anticipated.

Several miles passed without much activity. Occasionally, someone would crawl out of the ground and follow, or being too fleshless, took ghostly shapes and fell in line with the army of the undead.

Gert would occasionally talk with the "new recruits," Mitch noticed. He could understand them if he concentrated, but at this point, he was on a mission and trusted Gert was explaining the upcoming encounter as well as they both understood it.

Mitch noticed, with some degree of trepidation, that as he moved along the river, a foggy mist formed and remained over the water seemingly following them.

He stopped, it stopped. He moved faster, it moved faster. Probably just a trick of orientation and light. Or, at this point, Mitch thought arrogantly, 'It could be the devil's breath. If it's that, even the devil is scared to come too near me!'

This gave him a scale-tipping added degree of self-confidence. 'No going back now. Nothing can shock me. I am the Oniaten, and I….' His thoughts were suddenly interrupted by the sound of a heavy flop in the mud puddle to the right of his horse, causing it to rear up, but it settled right back down at Mitch's insistence.

Gert and the others, also alerted by the new, loud, flopping noise, looked up. None particularly concerned it appeared.

Mitch backed his horse up a bit and looked to his right, toward the river and its ever-present mist. He looked farther down and found a very pale man, completely devoid of clothing, but more than clothed in mud.

To Mitch's amazement, the man jumped up and wiped at the mud on his face and said, "And exactly who or what in the bloody hell are you anyway?" with an accent that would place him from the south end of London, Mitch conjectured.

Mitch looked at him for a full second or two and said, "Says the very pale, naked man who dropped out of the sky damn near killing me and hurting my horse?"

Mitch paused. "Since you asked first, I am Captain Mitch Garrett of the Revolutionary Colonial Army. And now, you are? And one more quick question, what is with the hair?" The newcomer's hair was greased into spikes that stuck out from his head like multiple horns.

"Somehow I think your horse was in more danger than you were," the muddy, pale man muttered almost to himself as he attempted, futilely, to brush away the mud. Then he said loudly to Mitch, "My name is Elrich." He bowed in an overly dramatic fashion that both annoyed and amused Mitch.

"I was travelling to dine with three young ladies I heard have just now arrived at the French town to the south. I hear one of them is from Italy, and I've always wanted to try that."

The pale man smiled, trying to hide his fangs but failing to notice the soil between him and the river had begun to virtually come to life; writhing, perhaps, the better description.

"And the hair thing?" Mitch asked again.

"Oh, yeah, bear grease; keeps the mosquitoes away. Can't stand those little bloodsuckers." He laughed a very awkward laugh.

Gert leaned toward Mitch and said, "Interestingly enough, Mitch, we call them undead bloodsuckers; not sure how that translates to English though."

From the man in the puddle, Mitch heard, "Undead bloodsuckers? Really? Undead bloodsuckers? I am a vampyre of one of the oldest families in these colonies. When you say vampyre, you better be pronouncing that 'y.'"

"Again, I ask no longer who you are, but what you are? Nothing I know of on this earth can bring me from bat to vampyre form without my intention."

Mitch could tell from Elrich's tone this was a sensitive thing to him, and at this point, he was killing a little time for Dieke and the rest to catch up. He pointed behind Elrich where the moving ground had started to give up its dead; some bones, some bones with attached skin and flesh, some just ghostly images of who they used to be. They also seemed to line up and begin to intone: OH-NEE-OTTON over and over toward Mitch. The ghostly troupe who had traveled with Mitch and Gert joined in, and Gert had to stop himself from joining in, as well.

Elrich looked from them to Mitch with a wry smile. Mitch motioned for the undead warriors to stop, and they did.

"Name's Mitch Garrett, you say, huh?" Elrich asked.

"Oh, sorry, forgot to mention that the locals tend to call me Oniaten."

When he spoke the name, his name, at least in part, the entire world jolted to those who were near. Even the mist rolled back away from the river which, itself, seemed to run backwards for a moment.

"Well, I'll be damned; again, that would be, I guess, but I thought the story of the Oniaten was a myth. Ironic from a vampyre, don't ya' think?"

Elrich looked hopefully into Mitch's eyes for a bit of humor. Seeing none, he said, "Well, as I said, I have some dinner reservations to get to."

Mitch, or rather the Oniaten, again bristled at the term "reservation," but in context, it seemed appropriate. "I hope you have clean clothes and a place to bathe when you arrive."

Elrich ran his hand along his still-mud-covered body and said, "With a body like this, who needs clothes? And as for the shower?" He ran toward the river, past the corporeal and incorporeal combined, and dove into the river at a place Mitch knew was not deep enough for him to dive into.

Apparently, Elrich's physics were good enough, for as his body hit the water, he melded into his bat form and emerged from the water wet but clean and flying south.

"Well, his bathing is all taken care of. Something makes me think we might see him again, Gert."

Gert nodded and said, "Or more like him anyway." He arranged the new spectral army into its adjusted battle groups, then suddenly looked to the left, away from the river.

Capricia

The trek from Pennsylvania through New York had taken nearly a month. Lady Capricia Fonterelli was beyond words with relief. Her two ladies-in-waiting, who had accompanied her on her trip, were not the greatest conversationalists. 'But then again, that was not the true purpose for keeping them around, was it?' she asked herself.

Their initial journey was a very hasty one. The locals had started to put two and two together and, more worryingly, started sharpening stakes of wood.

Lady Capricia was certainly not oblivious to the undead presence somewhere nearby, glancing at the beautiful bat briefly. That was a good indication that no one here was sharpening stakes…yet….at least.

'It had been peaceful in Pennsylvania,' Capricia reflected, 'for over fifty years.' Then she had gotten a little full of herself. "Bravado," her people called it, and someone had witnessed her crime.

In the dead of night, they had fled west toward the French town, where they had been invited by the owner of the local boarding house. A monsieur Francois LeBlanc.

It seemed Mr. LeBlanc owed her father, Count Luigi Fonterelli, a favor.

For what? The possibilities alone caused a shiver, even from Lady Capricia.

Mr. LeBlanc met the contingency as they reached the front door. He exchanged some pleasantries with the contessa, as he called her.

Capricia immediately turned to him, and with glowing eyes, said, "Never use contessa. You call me Lady Capricia, or do not call me at all!"

Properly corrected their host began to show the three of them their suite.

Just before reaching their rooms, Capricia, in a common moment of premonition, grabbed Francois by the shirt and whispered, "Someone might come to see me and my consorts soon. When they arrive, do be so kind as to show them in."

Francois smiled and nodded in eager agreement.

'The undead can be a very social group; a very small group,' Capricia had to admit to herself.

Mr. LeBlanc bowed slightly and said, "As you wish, counte…I mean my lady. Please send my kindest regards to your father."

She assured him his regards would be conveyed with her next correspondence.

Elrich II

The earlier conversation back at the tavern found the four vampyres had continued their drinks. Vampyres could, in fact, get drunk, but the amounts required were astronomical.

Elrich, at least, was not going to let drunkenness spoil his plans for the night.

"Three hours till darkness," he said out loud, more or less to himself, although the other three nodded at the obvious statement, each with their own plans for the night.

Elrich began to sip his ale rather than guzzle as he had been.

'Nothing is going to stop me from meeting the new girls!' This time he spoke it to himself.

Elrich And Capricia

Capricia looked out the window and noticed the sun had set, just beyond the swamps of the West. "Shan't be long, I think, till our visitor arrives."

The pale girls sitting on the settee behind her nodded, as always, in agreement.

The always-prescient Capricia was as accurate as ever, and less than an hour after darkness came a ring at the boardinghouse porch. She could hear the brief conversation:

Mr. LeBlanc: "May I help you, sir?"

Visitor: "Yes, I have heard that there are some ladies new to your town, and I would like to introduce myself and offer to show them around, as it were."

"Oh, the Contessa, I mean Lady Capricia," as if just remembering, "said someone one might come to see her this evening. Please remain here while I inform her of your presence."

Elrich nodded, more out of shock than agreement. 'How could anyone know I was coming…it was that damn 'Oh-Nee-otton,' I bet,' he said, trying out the word and waiting for any fallout from it being spoken aloud.

Sensing none he continued, 'Or better yet,' he thought, 'maybe my mere presence gets the ladies interested?' He internalized without as much sarcasm as could have been applied.

Mr. LeBlanc returned down the stairs and said, "Lady Capricia will meet you at the upper landing." He pointed to the stairs leading up to the lodging rooms.

With some degree of trepidation, Elrich slowly ascended the stairs. There was a sharp left turn at the top that led to a landing, where he viewed what was the most beautiful being he had ever not just seen but imagined.

In well over one hundred years, he had looked for such a woman. Looking into her eyes, he knew immediately that she already knew that.

Pale as porcelain was the most perfect face he had ever seen. Her low-cut, formal bustier showed an abundance of womanhood Elrich had only imagined, considering the barely surviving women on these outposts he had to choose from. Her hips were brought out beautifully by the flowing and slightly transparent skirt.

He shook his head, as if to get the ethereal image out of his mind. The image remained the same. "Wow," he said aloud, not meaning to.

She smiled, knowing that would have to be the response.

He did, however, notice upon looking again on her seemingly bloodless face the fangs that she was deliberately displaying, ruining his first thoughts, but causing a whole new set of thoughts to run through his mind.

'Run!' was his first thought, and a new one to him since his turning. He then came to himself and said internally, 'This changes things; not sure I am up for this after the colonial-Indian-specter thing but, hell, I'm here now. Might as well make a go of it.'

He bowed and said, "Thank you for the audience, my lady."

Capricia, obviously amused, not just by the gesture, but by the spiked blond hair, smiled and curtsied in response.

"Hello, and audience is not what I would call this…*awkward* is what I would call this," she said, displaying an even larger smile.

"So, my friend, you came for blood. Maybe some exotic food?" She then whispered into his ear, "I've had way too much English food to even consider you exotic, but your hair style fascinates me. Tell me why you look like a wet porcupine."

"Bear grease. Put it in your hair, and it will keep the mosquitoes, those little bloodsuckers, away," Elrich responded.

"A vampyre worried about blood suckers?" She laughed deeply, perhaps too deeply, Elrich sensed. But with each laugh her ample breasts rose and fell, and he searched his mind for anything else humorous he could say.

Elrich blushed, as much as a vampyre can, from a pale white to more of an off-white.

'Perhaps someone would call it antique-white someday,' Capricia thought. She had to admit she had a knack for color coordination, and if not for being an undead vampyre, could perhaps do interior decorating in years to come.

As Elrich came into the entryway, more of a large room, really, he could see just a glimpse of a pale, red-headed girl sitting on a couch in a room off of the one he and the lady were in.

Capricia noticed his observation and said, "Well, might as well get the introductions out of the way now." She walked toward what turned out to be a bedroom with a couch against the far wall.

Elrich noticed the bed was large enough for three, perhaps even four, people to sleep comfortably on. His thought for a minute was interrupted by Capricia saying and motioning toward the girls. "These are Amelia and Ophelia; they are my attendants." Elrich also noticed the emphasis on the "my" part.

She walked him farther down the hall, off the landing and to her suite of rooms. He also noticed the young girls appeared to be twins; very pale, about twenty with reddish hair and a strange smile on their faces. 'Almost like they were drugged,' he thought

"Amelia and Ophelia? Real names?" Elrich asked.

"I have no idea honestly; it's what I call them and what they answer to. They were a gift to me to repay my father for past considerations." She continued without interruption, "They are my sustenance and are off limits to you." She gave him a look and showed her ample fangs again.

Having noticed his view of the bed, she added, "They sustain me in every way I need, especially on the long trips to these lonesome western outposts." She raised her skirt a little and winked at Elrich.

Elrich did his best blush impersonation again and quickly said, "Well, I just wanted to welcome you to town and let you know you weren't alone."

'Sure, you did,' Capricia thought.

"I think I am going to head down to the inevitable battle between the colonials or revolutionaries, or whatever they are calling themselves these days. A bunch of undead native people and the British," Elrich said.

"Seems this one chap has become the Oniaten, yet introduced himself as Captain Michael? Markus? Mitch, that's it. He insisted his name was Captain Mitch Garrett," he continued as Capricia suddenly stared into the space behind him. "But the undead army he was raising were most definitely calling him Oniaten (he sounded the word out as before), over and over again."

Capricia, her head spinning at the mention of Mitch Garrett, felt a sense of fear that no vampyre ever wants to feel.

After a moment, she also feared Elrich had noticed, but she saw he was busy staring at her hand maidens. She thought this was, perhaps, the most apt term, because 'hand, neck, etc. maidens' hadn't been used yet.

She quickly regained her composure and asked. "Where is this battle you believe will happen to take place? I might like to stretch my legs later on this evening."

She, of course, stretched out a partially clothed and perfectly shaped leg to add emphasis and to further distract this vampyre, who was quickly starting to bore her. The information he had could mean her existence, so for now, she was stuck pretending to at least tolerate him.

"It's about twenty miles north from here. There is no way a horse could get you…" he trailed off. "Of course, you are a vampyre and will not be needing a horse; sometimes I am actually stupider than I think I am."

'I bet you are never as stupid as I think you are,' Capricia said in her head, but smiled and said, "Nonsense. Just tell me how to get there. A little live action theatre is what I need tonight."

After he had told her everything he knew, for some reason, she showed him to the door. At this point, he was more than willing to go, as he was clearly out of his league and kind of regretted the entire trip.

He went down the stairs, and Mr. LeBlanc kindly showed him out. He got out of lanternlight, hid the clothes, and went to bat form. At least he would see a battle tonight, and perhaps he could see Capricia again.

With the departure of the common vampyre, Capricia went into the bedroom and fed first on Emelia, who moaned a lovely moan as just enough blood was taken from her to keep her in her morphine-like state, as Ophelia stroked Capricia's hair and her neck, gently kissing her ear as she sucked on the moaning Emilia.

Stopping just where she needed to, she turned to Ophelia, who kissed her deeply and then offered her own neck in return.

There would be more, much more later, but right now, Capricia needed strength to change her form, get to this battle, and see this Oniaten, this Mitch Garrett, to try to mitigate the damage of years past maybe?

'I just hope I am not away from these two reprobates long enough to allow them to burn something else down. Good thing they're cute and European,' Capricia thought.

Tat'lani

She had been through these same woods, more or less this same trail, thousands of times, over thousands of years. So long, in fact, that the trees and other fauna had completely changed.

The weather was now warmer. Even the animals had changed drastically since her first trip here so many moons ago.

The hundred-mile journey that she had just travelled only involved avoiding three, small bears. Her very first time alone she had had to kill three just to get through, and those bears were three times the size. 'Mukwa, I believe the locals still called them,' she thought, smiling knowingly. 'Supposedly there was an ancient immortal one still in existence.'

Being undead herself left her little ability to doubt the story's validity openly, having seen the aftermath of some of the stories reassured her of the locals' belief of such, even if she had actually needed it.

'Must be the warm weather making these bears so weak and small,' she reasoned to herself.

She was getting close to the source of what was leading her, calling her. She recognized the familiarity the moment he re-entered existence.

Another like her, an old friend and ally, but also more.

Oniaten he had been called but had not been heard or felt by her for many generations.

She knew this particular call was important; she had heard it and had immediately started to travel here from what must have been over two hundred miles away; well past where the English men had dared to go, at least so far.

It made her a little nervous still to be near the white men, even though she could easily kill any or all of them, and they could do nothing to her that would last. Still, she knew the damage they had caused her people since their arrival a mere three hundred-odd years ago.

Despite her cautious nature, the need for revenge overruled, and she felt this would be an opportunity to repay a few debts.

Her appearance had changed through the millennia to blend in with each tribe she had joined; many of whom no longer existed.

She had also learned the fine art of being able to lie convincingly and in any native language in existence, as well as those that no longer did.

Her current appearance she had crafted after seeing the white man's paintings of their ideal Indian maiden and had reluctantly adopted it for the area she was in.

Her hair in braids, her leather tunic cut too high to protect her legs, legs free of hair, and showing more bosom than she really felt was necessary or comfortable.

She considered it a burden, but she had to admit she had the physique to pull it off. More than convincingly, which she had used to her advantage on many an occasion.

Being made immortal at twenty made you twenty forever, and the advantages of that far outweighed the "burden."

The only things about her that were not in the white man's image of the "maiden" were the war paint she wore on her face and the long-bow and quiver slung across her shoulder. 'Oh, and the spear might seem a little out of place, as well,' she mused to herself.

She paused at the crest of a small hill that overlooked one of the many river trails she had known in her life. She could see the river and the mist just coming in from the west.

She knew a harbinger when she saw one and knew the Oniaten was very near. The hairs on her head stood up as if about to be struck by lightning, and her braids, almost appearing as horns as they reached toward the source of the power.

She felt a charge within her; not sexual excitement, but the excitement of living, something she had not felt since she really was twenty and very much alive.

She finally caught a glimpse of the Oniaten, in the guise of a blue-coated soldier it appeared, but Tat'Lani could see the Oniaten within. She also noticed what appeared to be a medicine man on another horse, though an undead one. 'That will be a story I imagine,' she thought to herself.

She began to move through the dense underbrush toward to road to see what excitement lay ahead.

The medicine man seemed to notice her first, as the Oniaten, in this form, was busy talking to a naked white man who had just flown off as a bat. "Another interesting story I bet," she said silently.

From Gert's perspective:

Through the dense woods came an undead warrior, fully armed and in war paint. If it were not for his current status, Gert would have assumed her a living thing.

She was the most beautiful un-living thing he had ever seen. Thanks to his current condition, it should save an awkward greeting.

"Gert, are we prepared to move forward?" Mitch asked. Receiving no answer, he turned and looked to Gert, whose gaze led him to the form of the young female warrior who approached from the dense undergrowth.

This time the Oniaten asked her, "And what would your name be, young warrior?"

She squeaked at first, coughed dust from her throat, and said, clearly and strongly, "I am Tat'Lani of the Potawatomi tribe, most recently." She looked at herself and felt her stomach.

Mitch had noticed that and said, "And you have recently died, my dear, very recently from your appearance? Do you remember who did this to you?"

Gert, mouth still agape, just stared at her.

"Not my first death, but a British soldier preparing for departure thought he wanted to 'take' a native, to 'rape' me, in their terms. I slashed his throat. In his fall, he shot me here…" She pointed to her now-healed stomach.

The Oniaten noticed her words, accent, and remembered her from thousands of years before.

But allowing her to tell her story without correction, recognizing that this relative, no matter how old, was important to them all.

Gert now bellowed to the assorted undead army, "We kill every man in a red coat."

Mitch started to stop him, but the Oniaten in him made it impossible.

The assorted mob screamed, screeched, whispered, or mouthed their support.

Tat'Lani said, "I will take the lead now…It's more than war and your chief now; it's personal!" Then, as an afterthought, she said, "If it pleases the Oniaten."

The Oniaten noticed she had determined their mission without even being told, had pronounced his name perfectly, and also knew her words true, it was personal.

Gert started to protest, and Mitch looked back at him and shook his head. Saying quietly, "The Oniaten thinks this a good idea!"

Another hour was spent in rounding up troops along the route, getting the dirt out in some cases, and getting them to understand what they were to do and how they could help.

Mitch overlooked his new army. Not a bloody one of them alive, but he knew he could not be responsible for their deaths. Their chief's life was all he could, and needed to, concentrate on.

Capricia II

Capricia chose her favorite guise. Bats were very common but also potential victims to the many predatory birds in the area. If Elrich fell to such a fate, she would not be upset or surprised.

Her favorite guise was a black cougar, fairly common in these areas and rarely fired upon by the locals as long as they weren't raising livestock.

While black cougars were not a norm for vampyre forms, Capricia took the black cat ability literally and formed the biggest one she could find.

She could run up to thirty miles per hour on a level, open surface, and even through dense woods better than twenty.

She figured with Elrich's sense of direction and overall intelligence, they should get there about the same time. He had been gone about twenty minutes.

She kissed the girls goodbye, checked in with Mr. LeBlanc to make sure they would be fed again (soup and bread would be good), and walked out of the house and out of the lanternlight.

The moonlight could not help but reveal her naked form as she shed her dress and hung it safely in a high branch of the tree she was in front of.

If anyone had been watching, they would have seen a perfectly shaped woman's form turn into a perfectly shaped cougar's form.

With that she was off and running through the forest at an amazing speed, not just un-worried by the birds of prey but scaring them all from their roosting places. This was not dinner; this was something that dines on us, she could feel them think collectively.

Upon her arrival at the small, ghostly contingent, Capricia noticed the leader of the undead native crew was a woman…and quite a woman indeed. Surely this was new or Elrich would have gone on about her. She did know enough to heed Elrich's advice about staying away from the Oniaten as to remain in cat form; however, as she looked up the road to the west, she could see the glow…and then the beautiful man who had become the embodiment of this Oniaten and was instantly in love.

She shook her huge, feline head and thought, 'You are responsible for his parents' death. This can never work; what in the hell are you thinking?'

She was trying to work that out when she noticed another colonial soldier approach Mitch. His back was to her, but she still felt she might know him. Then he turned, and in her feline eyesight, just by the light of the moons, showed his face.

She froze. 'I came all this way to escape the only witness to what those people did, and I find him here, talking to the Oniaten." She looked at the blue-coated Oniaten, who was still the most handsome thing she had ever seen. 'This has to be a nightmare. I must make this right before I am killed. I am tired of running, and this feels like home. His parents supported me, and they were mere humans. Surely this undead offspring of theirs will be as kind.

'Avoid the other guy at all costs until this is solved,' she said in her currently cougarlike mind.

From other eyes, the army appeared as some ghostly forms, seemingly fully formed, fully dressed, and most completely see-through; awesome for fear, bad for battle.

Then there were the skeletal warriors, held together by will and hate and the Oniaten, still able to throw a spear or fire a bow, in some cases.

There were the newly undead, those still mostly intact who would and could carry and fire a gun. Some could swim in certain circumstances and tackle in almost all cases.

The term zombie was not one unfamiliar to her from her days farther south, but not one she thought would ever be uttered again, especially here.

Yet there they were…zombies. Perhaps a thousand, perhaps more.

The fifteen or so minutes spent dealing with the dandy vampyre allowed Mitch the ability to form his contingent just outside of the torchlight of the British departure point.

Allowing him to do so without being seen, as darkness fell.

They would form a line here until the army arrived.

He had Gert send out the 'spectral force' to do reconnaissance and report back before the fire power showed up.

The Shallows
Chapter Sixteen

It took just about fifteen minutes for both the reconnaissance team and the actual army to arrive at Mitch's point of observation.

Dieke halted his dystopian band of angry men who either wanted their chief back and/or everyone wearing a redcoat dead.

At this moment, that alone worked to Dieke's advantage. This was still new territory for him. Somewhere in the back of his mind, he knew it was new territory, period, and to just deal with it.

Gert came toward them and silently motioned them to either side of the river road.

Dieke could now see the light of the torches from the British post. Once pulled aside, Dieke whispered to Gert, "Where is Mitch?"

A soft voice behind him, undoubtedly Mitch's, said, "Always close by Gert, remember?"

Neither Gert nor Dieke seemed impressed by the levity.

Mitch continued, "We have a new undead warrior to lead the assault. You are to follow her orders if she issues them. You are not to interfere with her in any way," Mitch said to the stunned gathering. "Okay?"

After an extended pause, the nods of yes started to appear. "Alright, then, here's the plan…"

After the plan was relayed, the two armies separated. Dieke, as directed, had climbed to the top of what could almost be called a hill and observed the redcoat preparations for departure.

Their force had obviously not been spotted by the enemy, for no eyes were cast anywhere near their direction. Every British eye was on the waterfront, beyond that, the warships in the great lake, or the tasks laid before them.

There were easily a thousand troops lined down the territorial road to the south. Many wagons loaded, some with ordinance some with other supplies.

To Dieke's interest, they seemed to be destroying the wagons and any materials they could not get on the small evacuation boats and rafts they had to use to navigate the shallows out to the big lake and the battleships beyond.

'Be nice to save a few of those for ourselves,' he thought. He considered rushing them but stuck with the plan.

Thirty men at a time, Dieke estimated, were leaving the shore. 'We can take them after they make another three hundred trips or so,' he thought despondently.

His attention was drawn to his left, across from the troops, and up the north territorial road; first a glow and then the clear sound of feet on the ground.

Around the bend came an amazing display of light and gore, led by the living dead in black cloaks, waving burning braziers, and Mitch and Gert on horses just behind them.

They approached the crossroads at the river in front of Dieke and beckoned him down from his "hill."

Dieke, while awed by the spectacle, was a bit reassured when he noticed the British apparently did not see them.

As part of the agreed upon plan, Mitch and Gert had in the meantime headed north with the new army of the undead that had been assembled, still picking up "volunteers" along the way. They used trails long overgrown from decades, if not centuries of disuse, made even more real by the appearance of some of the new warriors who had joined their growing army.

"We should meet up with the territorial road just up here," Gert said to Mitch, pointing to his right. "There used to be a French mission here; be careful, there might be a cemetery."

"Why should I care about a French cemete—" The word was lost as the soil began to move and black cloaked forms, mostly with flesh Mitch thought hopefully, rose from the ground.

"Don't worry, Mitch," Gert said, "the British killed them for enabling us… the natives, that is."

"So, they should be on our side?" Mitch asked.

"You brought them back to life; they should always be on your side," Gert said as he helped the last two from their graves. The last one Gert pulled from his internment, a Father B. Ringuette, if his grave marker was any indication, kissed Gert's hands and thanked him, asking, "Which angel are you, dear boy?"

"I'm Gert," he said.

"Oh," Father Ringuette said. "Don't remember you but, hey, never look a gift angel in the face, they say."

"Do they say that?" Gert asked.

"Well, they will now, won't they, lad?" what was left of father Ringuette rasped as he slapped Gert on the back.

"Let's get these incense things cleaned off and working as soon as possible," Gert shouted. Many of the undead rose to the occasion to help Gert in this matter.

Mitch motioned Gert over and asked, "Why is it so important for the incense things, I believe you called them, to get going…is it part of the magic?"

"No, Mitch," Gert smiled. "Maybe you can't smell a thousand dead bodies marching in step, but this undead fellow can! Plus, it will bring an extra scare to the Brits. Make sure Dieke doesn't fire on us. If he follows the plans, he will be expecting us, maybe without the aroma, but he shouldn't fire unless he hears me or Tat'Lani order it."

The "eyes" stared on in wonder, though from a slightly different perspective, in confusion and in utter amazement at what could so easily be done with so little.

'Perhaps human survival instincts remained, even with their desperate need for revenge.

Perhaps revenge itself is a means of survival. Best not to share that with those of my own kind,' it thought, 'unless and until necessary. Let's hope it never is.'

Yet another set of "eyes" stared on in mild interest, understanding fully what could be wrought with very little. 'Humans are still a strong and equal force but have a memory which will be their undoing. Feelings, for themselves and others, can be exploited, I must share this with my own kind…NOW!'

Chapter Seventeen

Mitch and Dieke's forces finally met at the lowland of the territorial road, just out of view of the redcoats. The sun was fully set now, one full moon, and one, a half moon, just about to rise.

Dieke looked up the road to the north and had to ask Mitch, "Where in the hell did you pick up the dead bloody priests?"

"Cemetery, where else?" Mitch said. "Gert thought the incense made the trip nicer. Can't say I disagree."

As they spoke, the spectral reconnaissance team arrived. The chief was to be loaded on the second boat to return from the Warship HMS Queen Anne. The specter motioned out into the deeper part of the river, to the battleship closest to shore.

Gert looked around for Tat'Lani. He could barely make out her glow, and she moved closer to the water and the battle.

Gert mentioned that a local had told him the other two ships farther out were the HMS Mercy and HMS Trower, also warships but way too far out for their guns to reach shore. Even the Queen Anne would be taking out as many of her soldiers as any others firing to shore at this range.

As if on a dare, a cannon ball landed close to the point of departure for the British.

"None of us are even in that area. What the hell is going on?" Dieke asked.

The spectral army marched forward, past even Mitch.

'STOP!' the Oniaten said. They stopped. Another impact landed near the departure point.

"Gert, what in the hell is happening here?" Mitch screamed over the cannon blasts from the ship.

Gert shrugged, "Only one way to find out, Captain. To the new warrior army he yelled "FORWARD!"

The force of the undead marched toward the fork and the path to the shallows, with Gert at its lead, yet still at least one hundred yards behind Tat'Lani, who was already swimming into the shallows.

Dieke, on the left, gave similar instructions to his men close by.

"If you want me to continue leading this army from here on, Mitch, you really need to stay close to me!" Gert said, the irony not lost on Mitch, who moved his horse to accompany this marching mass of morbidity.

"And for the love of the elders, do not let me lose. I mean *us* lose Tat'Lani, what a force she is!" Mitch nodded and completely understood. Completely understood indeed.

Close to the fork and the shallows departure area, Mitch and his assorted clan saw what the Queen Anne was firing on.

Thousands of, in most cases spectral, carcasses in others, native warriors appearing to stand all over the shore, all around the British soldiers.

Quite frankly everywhere.

Gert yelled something in a language Dieke did not understand, but 'attack' sounds very similar in any language.

The undead natives ran headlong toward the waiting redcoats, being blown to pieces along the way; however, Dieke noticed it didn't seem to slow them down much unless they lost a limb, and even then, they kept coming at the British soldiers.

Dieke ordered, "All troops to sharpshooter positions!" As per the plan, all living soldiers under Captain Dieke Carson assumed sharpshooter positions, picking off redcoats as they ran from the relentless cannon fire of their own ship, firing upon phantom natives they could see but never kill.

Mitch saw above the fray the British with Colonel Timmons on board desperately trying to get Chief Quay Quay into a new relief boat out past the shallows; the last one having been damaged in the Queen Anne's relentless and yet fruitless fire.

As he was brought aboard this last ship, several glowing canoes with skeletal crews closed in on the relief boat.

Chief Quay Quay, realizing his new position of escape, jumped from the British boat toward one of the glowing canoes he hoped would hold his weight, despite its years of burial… guessed wrong… but was pulled up out of the muck by Tat'Lani, who in unceremonious roughness, grabbed the chief around the waist and swam desperately for shore.

Finally, a newer enough canoe was found, and he was hoisted into and landed safely at the foot of the bones of a great warrior, still wearing his headdress. Tat'Lani clung to the side, her breath steady, eyes sharp.

The skeleton smiled at Quay Quay, if that was possible, and said, "I will bring you to the Oniaten now."

Tat'Lani treaded water and held the canoe and the chief's hand all the way back to shore.

Timmons and those left on the relief ship rowed as quickly as possible to the Queen Anne.

Almost as one, every undead fighter looked to Mitch to see what they should do.

Mitch, in a moment he would later fear a weakness, just motioned them back to shore.

The chief being returned was the goal, after all.

It was decided that Dieke and the other colonial soldiers would march the British prisoners back toward the main force of the Continental army, now nearing the French town on the River Raison, and turn them over to be welcomed as heroes, however undeservedly. No one was going to tell their superiors what had really happened. They had all agreed upon it; it was settled.

The British gone, dead, or captured would be 'little trouble to anyone again for a few years anyway,' Mitch hoped as much as he thought.

What the Oniaten thought was a whole different matter.

Post log:

Going Home Again?

The trip back toward the camp consisted of returning warriors back to their burial places, their work, for now, done.

As they approached the place Tat'Lani had appeared, she spoke to Gert and the Oniaten: "I was not killed in a battle of nations but of two people. I was never given a proper burial. I would like that, at least." she looked at Gert from the corner of her still clear eyes.

Mitch thought this appropriate, and it made sense to him.

The Oniaten knew Tat'Lani was as old as him, if not older. It was not he who had raised her from the dead; she had been undead for millennia.

Yet still knew she would be an aide for as many years, and Gert was obviously taken with her. Her lie would serve her and himself well and make Gert the happiest undead medicine man on earth.

In doing so, Mitch could allow Gert to be the hero he wanted to be.

As if on cue: "Or…." Gert said, "you could return with us? You just have to stay fairly close to the Oniaten." Motioning to Mitch, he said, "I obviously have to, so I would be happy to show you how."

Gert looked to Mitch, and then through him to the Oniaten, and both agreed that a powerful female warrior would be a big help in raising the girls of the tribe to the positions of power they could achieve. At the least, Mitch realized, Gert could believe he could find a mate for all eternity, and if she got tired of him, she knew how to take care of herself.

"Very well, Tat'Lani," Mitch said, "you are one with us."

Very clearly the Oniaten said, 'Welcome to the Mukwa clan…more or less forever.'

KT And Capricia

KT heard the soft feminine "hello" come from outside the longhouse door currently occupied by Jethro, her grandfather, and herself. Jethro immediately rose to the voice, but KT motioned him to sit.

She opened the flap just a little and saw a naked European woman, dark features, not likely a local.

She stepped outside and closed the flap behind her.

"Can I help you?" she asked, waving her hand over Capricia's naked body. Capricia smiled and in no way tried to hide herself, KT noticed which, along with her appearance alone made things a little strange.

"Is this where the Oniaten resides?" Capricia asked with some hesitation.

KT, feeling a little more comfortable with what the situation was, now said, "Yes, my dear, or somewhere near. He should be back shortly. Can I get you something to wear?"

KT again pointed out Capricia's nakedness, and after too much reflection KT felt, Capricia said, "Yes if you have a cloak or something, that would probably be better." Looking down at herself, unconvinced, but realizing a subject of convention.

KT came out with an appropriately revealing cloak Capricia could just tie at the waist and feel free to spin and sit as she chose.

Far be it from KT to judge another woman's methods, as she had used her own with Dieke so recently.

As Mitch and the group that was left reached the gates of the reservation, he quite clearly saw a dark, maybe even exotic, European woman in what appeared to be native clothing, looking quite anxious and waiting apparently desperately to see him or someone from his small party of followers. She was jumping up and down, which also did not go unnoticed.

The closer he got to her, the more he thought he liked the idea of her wanting to see him. Also, the more of her he thought he might like to see.

'Hey,' Mitch thought, 'at least that part seems to be working, and who knows what powers it might possess now?' He chuckled to himself.

'They might not be anything special,' the Oniaten said. 'I don't know what powers you had before, just more magic in whatever tool you might possess. Sorry, lad, you will always be Mitch- sized.'

Tat'Lani had also noticed the dark-haired woman, and if facial indications were any clue, she had some of the same ideas.

As they approached, the young lady said, "I am Countess Capricia Fonterelli. Please just call me Capricia, and I would very much like an opportunity to talk with Mitch Garrett. I fully realize this will be attended by the Oniaten, as well."

It was then that Mitch noticed she, too, was undead and took his hat off and bowed from his seated position on his horse.

"I, or rather, *we* will be happy to speak with you in my quarters. Please give me a moment to put my horse away and get these folks," he motioned to the group, "back where they belong. Then I am all yours."

Capricia desperately hoped so!

With all living and dead in a set place, Mitch walked into the longhouse, gave an update to Chewachta and, of course, KT, who seemed particularly concerned about when Dieke would be back.

She seemed relieved that he was fine and was planning to return as quickly as possible since he was required to take the prisoners back the twenty-five miles or so to the French town.

Then, being led by KT, he went into a private house that had been built for the chief, who wanted to remain this night in the longhouse with Chewachta, Gert, and KT to catch up on recent events and such.

Before Mitch left, Chief Quay Quay reached his hand out to him.

Mitch went to take it as a handshake, but Quay Quay grabbed past his hand to his forearm and grasped it there. Mitch returned the gesture.

The chief met Mitch's eyes and said, "I welcome you, both of you. This," he motioned in a circle, "is your home for as long as you need."

The chief also explained, as best he could, that it was only fair the Oniaten should have first use of his special roundhouse.

Mitch, wasting no time, went to the chief's roundhouse.

Capricia had already been taken there. She seemed unable to wait until Mitch had fully entered the roundhouse to begin to talk. Her voice so fast, so melodious, that Mitch was almost lulled into a state of hypnosis…

As 'things' began to appear in Mitch's mind, there was an announcement from outside the tent: "Chief Quay Quay to see you. "Oniaten and Mitch, too, I guess." It was obviously Jethro's voice.

The illusion or dream stopped, and Mitch said after a moment, "Certainly. I always welcome the chief."

The chief was led inside and came straight to Mitch's face. He stared for a moment and said, "I forgot to give you this." He then pulled one of the eagle feathers from the elaborate decorations on his slim line of hair and placed it underneath the strap that held Mitch's tri-corner hat in place.

He bowed to Mitch and the Oniaten and backed slowly out of the roundhouse.

Sneak Peak from:

The Oniaten Book II: The Touchstone

Prologue

The guard had become spellbound by his prisoner's story, so much so that he could almost see the story as it was told. He also noticed that as he looked Mitch in the face, it was never a constant image. Sometimes there would be the wrinkles of an old man, and at times the skin irritation that the young suffer.

It took him several minutes to notice that Mitch had stopped talking and another to notice he was looking at him and smiling.

Confused and a little embarrassed the guard roared, "What? Why are you looking at me? What is so damned funny?"

Mitch patted the guard's shoulder again, the heavy chains rattling almost like the incessant voice of the old man in the next cell. "I was just watching your reactions to my story to make sure you were getting it. The smile was because I can see you are." Mitch said calmly and steadily. "It is getting a little dark in here, and I bet you're hungry." Mitch said to the guard. "Any chance we can continue this story over some food?"

The guard considered this, and thought a candle rather than a torch or a lantern would be more appropriate, and then immediately asked himself 'what the hell am I thinking?' He glanced back at Captain Garrett who continued smiling.

"I am required to feed you, and, I guess, I am hungry as well. Let me see what I can dig up for us. Your story alone is worth more than bread and water, and I would hate to eat beef in front of you." He snickered to himself, knowing that to be a lie in most cases. "I'll be right back," he said to Mitch. Exited and locked the cell door, the bolt slamming home a seeming punctuation mark to his words.

Left alone in almost non-existent light, Mitch, now fully aware of his surroundings called out "Gert?" I know you can't be far…" 'unless?' Mitch momentarily thought of the work it would be to go to every place they buried a body from the earlier battle, calling out 'Gert' like an owner looking for a lost dog. Only a dead one in this case. Just as he was finishing that thought he heard Gert just outside the window of the cell.

"Mitch is that you?" was what Gert was saying. "is that you Mitch?"

"No Gert, I am just some random guy they locked up who also has a friend named Gert who would be within earshot of a jail cell." This would seem a cruel degree of sarcasm, but Gert being a "Medicine Man", and generally a worker not a thinker, merely said, "Oh it is you, good."

Mitch could imagine the blank look on Gert's face that would have accompanied those words.

"Do you want me to get you out of there?" Gert asked.

"Not yet Gert. I am also sure you know, I could get out whenever I wanted to. Something about this guard makes me wish to know more, plus any information from the losing side will help us relay it to the tribes on our journey back home."

Gert standing in the dark alley behind the jail nodded in understanding. This too Mitch could picture, and that caused him even more of a smile.

"Well then can I come in?" Gert asked.

"There seems to be an older native in the cell next to mine, try to get in there, so you can hear better, plus seems the old man might need some assistance. Do wait though until the guard is back and in here with me, he appears to be the only one at this jailhouse." Mitch ended his instructions as the door once more violently opened. This time it was because the guard's arms were full of fresh bread, meats and cheeses. Not to mention a small candelabra with three lit candles. The food was a spread the likes of which Mitch had not seen since leaving Garretton some 5 months previously. The guard had used his oversized foot to open the door and apologized to Mitch for the noise.

Mitch waived him off, with the rattle of his chains making their own inharmonic melody. Mitch looked at them, then the guard and said. I could have helped you, but…" again he rattled his chains.

The Guard looked at the chains and at Mitch. 'He seems small and relatively harmless,' he thought. Then said, "I suppose one off would be OK, it will make it easier for you to eat."

"That would be fantastic, I thank you my good man." Mitch said with convincing emotion. As the guard engaged in removing his right-hand shackle, Mitch continued the conversation. "I feel at a disadvantage though." Feigning hurt feelings with a passing frown. "You seem to know all about me and I don't even know your name. Calling you 'Guard' seems a little too impersonal don't ya' think?"

"Oh, do forgive me," the guard said, surprised by his own words and tone of voice. He paused and tried to figure out why he was being so nice, then he looked at Mitch again, who had resumed his bucolic smile and said, "Well, my name is Morton, Morton Mathers. He patted his ample mid-section, smiled a broad welcoming smile and said; but my smart friends call me 'Slim'."

Mitch chuckled good naturedly and said, "then Slim it is, and please just call me Mitch. Slim reached out his hand, Mitch firmly, not too firmly he reminded himself, but firmly enough, took his hand and shook it.

As Slim and Mitch set out the food and placed the candles where they would be of most use, the croak from the next cell asked, "Do you have any extra food for me?" Mitch looked at the guard who appeared or pretended not to hear it.

Mitch asked Slim, "Has the old man in the next cell," he jerked his head indicating the cell next door, "been fed recently?"

Slim looked up at him and said dismissively, "We are the only two here. This is a jail that hasn't been used since the late '40's. But it was the closest one to the battle and you were the only survivor. Again," the guard turned toward Mitch saying, "under mysterious circumstances." He eyed Mitch with renewed wariness, but then smiled and said, "Speaking of mysterious circumstances, your story left off with the withdrawal of the Red Coats and the forming of a Treaty with the natives that had helped you? Right?"

"Oh yes," said Mitch in between bites of bread and dried meat, which, like all food now, was a little bitter. "And the story has just begun."